SHANIQUA'S WORLD

AN URBAN NOVEL

MPINGO UHURU

ZURI WORLD PUBLISHING

DEDICATION

First of all I wish to thank my publisher and friend Tio for taking a chance on me, and for giving me the opportunity to showcase my talent and share my dreams and voice with the world. I look forward to many more collaborations in the future.

To Key'maurie (KC 400), I love you! Thank you for being by my side through the thick and thin. No one knows what the future holds but I know that mine will be all the more brighter because you are in it.

Para mi hermana Billy: No hay palabras que nunca jamas puedan describir cuanto te amo. Tu llegaste a mi mundo y trajiste del sol a mi noche mas oscura. Tu amor y apoyo no tiene medido.

Gracias por darme mi familia: gracias por Jose, Merche, Marco, Papa Antonio, Mamen, Sonia, Sandra, Alberto, y Said y un amor especial y gracias a mama Pepa. Ella esta en mi corazón. Te amo hermana.

To my friend Caroline, I will forever be indebted to you and love you for your tireless work and effort on my behalf. You are my hero and I keep you in my heart at all times. Thank you for your love, support, and understanding. We got this! :)

Julia, nothing would ever make me forget you. Thank you for reaching halfway across the world to embrace me with your love and support. I can't wait to eat Black Forrest Cake with you. :)

Lastly, to all the haters and naysayers who have come and gone; I thank you! Because of your hate, I know love. Because of your anger and scorn, I know joy and happiness. Because of your discord, I now know peace. So, please continue to hate and be bitter. It makes my life all the more loving and sweeter.

CONTENTS

CHAPTER ONE

Shaniqua stretched out lazily on the plush king size bed. The silk sheets felt smooth and cool against her naked body. She admired her sexiness with an appreciative eye. She nodded her head approvingly at her five-seven, 36-24-40 frame. She had learned at an early age what a woman with a fine body, good looks, and a sharp mind could do to a man. She had been doing it since she was eleven years old.

Her mind was prevented from reliving her past as Ervin, her current conquest, as such as he was, climbed into bed next to her. Ervin Wilcox, big time bailer, finer than the average man had a right to be, stood at the height of six-two and weighed two hundred-thirty pounds with twenty-inch arms, a chest like a stallion and the looks of a god. He also had a penis the size of a toothpick.

Shaniqua looked at the disgusting little pull back thing as it pointed upwards from in between his legs. She felt a sudden sense of revulsion yet she swallowed it down. After all, Ervin was paying for her three-bedroom apartment, her new silver and black BMW 640 Gran Coupe, her endless shopping sprees and all of her bills. If having to deal with a small prick was the price she had to pay then she was willing to buckle down, fake all the oooh's and ahhh's that were needed to keep his dough rolling in.

Ervin smiled at her in an attempt at seduction then climbed on top of her, spread her legs apart then immediately started poking inside of her. In a matter of seconds, he was panting and sweating like a warthog in heat.

Shaniqua closed her eyes and did what she always did when having what passed for sex with Ervin. She thought about Shane.

Shane Wilcox was Ervin's younger brother by two years. He was twenty-two, smart as hell and could easily pass for Trey Songz's twin brother. He had a deep bass voice that made Shaniqua cream every time she heard it. And, that body, well, it made her salivate each time she was blessed to lay eyes upon him. He was Ervin's right-hand man and fiercely loyal to the game. He was also, Shaniqua knew, secretly in love with her.

The two of them rarely spoke for they were never together alone too often. Not that Ervin didn't trust her or his little brother, for he had no idea about Shane's crush on her or her lust for him. No, they were never alone together for long because Shane was always at his brother's side.

Well always except for times like these when Ervin would whisk her away on the spur of the moment. They were currently sharing what he believed was a romantic night in a downtown hotel. Shaniqua was just thankful that the night wouldn't be lasting long.

Just as she had Shane's sexy face imprinted in her mind, it

was washed away by the disgusting tongue bath Ervin called kisses. He coated her face with saliva and she could smell the foulness of his breath *f* and gritted her teeth to hold back her anger. Every time Ervin kissed her, she had an image of her face being assaulted by an army of slugs that once they had their way with her, they left a trail of thick ooze that dripped sticky from her every pore.

Shaniqua knew that Ervin considered himself to be a skilled and desirable lover yet she would have rather fucked a corpse than have to constantly endure the onslaught of his acts.

Ervin flicked his tongue inside her nostrils, effectively clogging them with his saliva, and the stench nearly made her gag. Her body jerked involuntarily.

Ervin in the heat of his lovemaking took her movements as a sign that his sex was intensely pleasing to her. He increased his speed. Shaniqua turned her head and just as she managed to clear her nose, Ervin farted.

"PPPPhhhhhhrrrraaattttttt!!!!!!!!"

Oh hell no! She thought as the smell of rotten eggs and week old garbage accosted her already overworked sense of smell. Thus nasty ass nigga didn't just fart on me! She found herself trying to squirm from up under him but Ervin gripped her hips and held her in place. He was on the verge of cumming.

Just as she felt as if she was about to die from his stench, Ervin grunted, shoved his foul-tasting tongue down her throat and exhaled with his release.

Without missing a beat, he rolled off of her, stood up and started scratching his ass. Before she could form a cohesive thought, he farted again.

It was at that point Shaniqua realized that she could not take anymore. FUCK IT!!!! She was done. Apartment, cars and shopping sprees be damned! She had spent the last three years of her life enduring his nasty ass and she knew she couldn't endure anymore.

Before Ervin could do so much as even look at her, she rolled off the bed and quickly retreated to the bathroom. She immediately locked the door and leaned her back against it.

As she looked at herself in the mirror, she was disgusted with the image that greeted her. Her long silky black hair was a matted mess. Gone were all traces of the three-hundred-dollar hairstyle she had paid her hairdresser Tanya for. Her body was covered in sweat yet every ounce of it belonged to Ervin, and her face looked as if she had just run inside out of a down pouring of rain. Ervin's tongue had effectively smeared her make up making her appearance look like something from a horror flick.

She jumped into the shower and let the hot water cascade over her body. Closing her eyes, she thought about her plight and the predicament she now found herself in. It wasn't that Ervin wasn't kind and generous to her for he was that and more. He and Shane ran some of the most lucrative drug rings in the entire city. They were making more money than most people could even imagine; Money that Ervin spent in quantities and all on satisfying her every whim.

The two of them had met when she was just nineteen. She had been at one of the local parks watching the neighborhood thugs as they ran up and down the basketball court with their shirts off, six packs showing and basketball shorts hanging halfway off their asses.

Shaniqua had just ended her relationship with her ex-boyfriend Raymond after catching him in an alley getting head form some doped out crack head who looked only moments from death. The woman was so covered in grit and grime, it was difficult to even recognize her as a female or any other species for that matter.

As Shaniqua sat watching all the hot and sweaty bodies deciding on which would become her next conquest, for that is exactly what she considered them, she sensed a presence watching her. She looked around quickly and pushed her hand into her new Versace bag, a gift to herself, and wrapped it around the handle of her little black .22. She had learned to carry it everywhere she went. After all, a girl couldn't be too careful. When she didn't notice anyone paying more than the usual attention to her, she turned back to the game.

In her mind, Shaniqua narrowed her choices down between two of the guys on the court. The first was Lance Bailey. Lance was five ten and weighed a good hundred and eighty-five pounds. He had smooth dark chocolate skin. He wore his hair cut low and always seemed to smile.

Even still, no one who knew him was fooled by it, for it was well known that Lance had a temper that would flash like lightning. He brokered no form of weakness. He couldn't. He was too involved in the gutters of the streets. He held down several blocks and sold the most crack, heroin, and weed on the entire north side. Plus, he was the head of a notorious and vicious crew that was ready to jump at his every word.

Shaniqua could see herself as his girl. She knew that not a single bitch in the entire city would even dare step to her. She also knew that Lance had a thing for her. She had observed him checking her out on the sly on several occasions. She noticed him even as he dribbled the ball admiring her from top to bottom.

Lance was stealing glances to see if she was looking and whenever they made eye contact, he would smile and show out that much more on the court side to Shaniqua. Nor did the fact that he also already had three other baby mamas and four kids. No, to her, all that mattered was that his pockets stayed fat and that he wanted her.

Shaniqua's second choice was someone she had known since she was seven years old. They had gone to the same church together. His name was Cory Peters.

Cory was a mutt. A mixed breed. He was half Hispanic and half black. He had greenish-grey eyes, long hair he kept in designed cornrows and a body every woman seemed to drool over. He was six-three yet chi sled and toned. He had what was known as a babyface and a voice that would easily make Tyrese, Usher, and Miguel stand up and take notice.

Although Cory wasn't involved in the drug game, he was still a major figure in the streets and moved with a lot of force. Cory was a gun runner. He sold any and every kind of gun you could think of. If he didn't have it, there was never a problem with getting it. He would simply contact his two uncles who served in the military and within a matter of hours, receive the package.

Cory didn't move with the familiar crowd of people. He ran in a different circle. Cory moved with the underground. That, in and of itself, wasn't all that appealing to Shaniqua, but she figured that she could grow used to it and or eventually, persuade Cory to move with the crowd that appealed to her.

She knew that he would for Cory had been crushing on her since day one. She had even allowed him to feel her up a few times. They had shared kisses yet nothing solid had ever come of it. Mainly due to the fact that Shaniqua was always moving to the beat of the streets and had no desire ever to slow down.

She was certain she would remain that way. Cory wanted the traditional, stay at home type of girl and she knew that she didn't and wouldn't fit that mold. But still...he had major clout and long paper.

Shaniqua hit the bleachers going back and forth between the two of them in her mind. Every time she felt that she had come to a conclusion, the other would shove his way back into competition. She sighed to herself then suddenly whipped her head around for she was sure that someone was hawking her.

She was right. Ervin stood not three feet away admiring the thick curves of her body that she had managed to squeeze into a pair of ass hugging designer jeans and a baby T-shirt.

Shaniqua did not know who he was but she could tell that he was an impact and somebody by the way Lance and Cory dropped the basketball game and walked over and acknowledged him. The three of them along with a few other players in the streets moved off a short distance and one by one, he worked business with them. The entire time, however, he kept his eyes on her.

Once he was done, he walked over, extended his hand and introduced himself.

Shaniqua's eyes fell on the platinum and diamond Rolex watch he wore on his wrist and the matching Rolex ring and chain. Her libido instantly perked. When she extended her hand and introduced herself, she assessed the strength of his handshake. When Ervin raised her hand and Lightly brushed his lips across it, she knew her choice had been made. They had been together since that day.

Well, it's time for shit to change! Shaniqua thought to herself. She ran the suds-filled loofa over her smooth, flawless, caramel skin and took pleasure in her sexiness. Unlike a lot of women, she embraced her sexy and had no qualms about using it to get whatever in the hell she wanted.

At twenty-two, she knew she was a knockout and beautiful enough to grace the cover of any magazine and fine enough to spotlight any video. Those two tor it video vixens she saw parading around on t.v. were a joke. Yes, she knew that she could do those things and more, but why should she?

There was a world full of men just waiting for the chance to be the one to satisfy her every desire. She didn't need to lift a finger and therefore, she wouldn't.

Still, she thought, I ain't got to put up with Ervin's tired ass! She didn't know how, but she knew that she needed, no, had to shake him. He had gone from being her prince charming to a common bullfrog. Hell, he even sounded like one every night when he snored.

Unbidden, her mind shifted back to Shane. Shane with his sexy smile, juicy lips and big dick. Oh, she knew he was hung, although she had never had any. She had seen it hanging out of his boxers one night when he had gotten so wasted, he had to stay over at her apartment.

Ervin refused to let Shane drive home that way. That night, she had wanted so badly to fuck Shane but was scared to even think about mentioning it let alone, trying it. If Ervin found out, she knew that she would have ended up in a hospital's emergency room somewhere clinging to life, or dead in a glitter mutilated beyond recognition.

Rinsing and drying off, Shaniqua took her time rubbing the Nivea Shea and cocoa butter lotion over her body. She then dabbed on a light scent of her channel, threw on a pair of sexy boy shorts and a large T-shirt, and stepped back into the bedroom.

Ervin was already sound asleep sprawled out naked across the bed. His snores echoed in the silent room. "Hell nav, this nasty ass nigga ain't even gone wash his stankin' ass?" Shaniqua mumbled softly.

She frowned then grabbed a quilt from the closet, stepped into the living- room area of the suite, settled on the sofa and curled up with the remote. She flipped through the channels but found nothing of interest. Clicking the t.v. off she lay back lost in thoughts of Shane and how she could have him. Just before she fell asleep, an idea formed in her mind.

CHAPTER TWO

"Girl that nigga gets me wet every time I see his fine ass," Tanya said while running the brush she held through Shaniqua's long hair. "I'm telling you, Inna get me a piece of that before long." Shaniqua laughed at the image of Tanya's face reflected in the mirror. Tanya's jaw was set in that determined fashion she always got when she had her mind set on something.

To say that Tanya's beauty was stunning would be not to give her just due. She was drop dead gorgeous. She stood an even five-eight, had long perfectly sculpted legs, an ass to make Beyonce and Shakira green with envy and perfect round tits. She was chocolate. A deep dark, rich, smooth chocolate. Her skin glowed radiantly and was without blemish. She wore her dark, auburn colored hair in a silky wave pattern that cascaded down her back. And, unlike many of her clients, her hair was 100% all natural and all hers.

Tanya joined Shaniqua in laughing, revealing her perfectly white teeth. She had deep African features, high cheekbones, dark hazel eyes, a small but wide nose, and moist plump lips that she kept glossed to a perfect shine. As with her lip gloss, the rest of her make-up and attire was immaculate.

Shaniqua marveled, like always at Tanya's perfectly pitched high voice, for to see and hear Tanya, no one would ever guess that she was a pre-op trans- gendered woman. She looked and carried herself as any cis-woman in the world would.

"What? Girl, I'm serious as hell! That fine ass nigga keep walking up in here looking at me like that, shit, I'd be a damn fool not to, and my mama ain't raise no fool."

"Yo mama ain't even raise yo' crazy ass, Tanya. Yo' grand-mama did!" Raena, the third person at Tanya's booth said. "And, she had more than a hand full with yo' ass." Once again, Shaniqua laughed.

They were talking about Cory. Once a week, he made his way into the shop to get his hair braided. That Tanya was the best hair stylist up in the place was not up for debate. She had more clientele than any two other stylists put together. And, she had a waiting list a mile long. Shaniqua knew that many people envied the fact that she was always first on Tanya's list.

Tanya had grown up with both Raena and her Teaming how to survive out in the streets. Tanya had had it worst out of them all. Her dad had left them when she was ten. It was also at that time in her life she had revealed to her mother that she was in fact, a girl and not a boy. Her mom reacted to the reve-lation by beating Tanya nearly senseless then throwing her out of the house. If it had not been for Tanya's grandmother, Ms. Uma, Tanya would Wave been completely out on the streets.

Tanya, like any ten-year-old, had thought her mother would come around and accept her for who she was. That never happened. Only three weeks after kicking Tanya out, her mother drowned in her own bathtub. Her mother's death was still a sore spot she bore within her every day.

"Well, both of y'all ain't got to worry cause I'm the only bitch Cory is interested in." Shaniqua finally said. Even though she had said it jokingly, she knew that it was true. After all, Cory had been desiring her all this time. The fact that he always left Tanya a large tip each time he came in, only went to show Shaniqua that he wasn't a tightwad.

"Whatever!" Raena snapped. She too knew that Cory wanted Shaniqua. That was fine by her. What got her, however, was the fact that Ervin had chosen Shaniqua over her. She had been pursuing that man for the longest. Although she never said anything to her girl about her desires, it still grated on her that he had chosen Shaniqua.

"Well, anyway," Tanya said. "What y'all got going tonight?" She put the final touches on Shaniqua's doo, then turned her around to face the mirror again. Shaniqua didn't bother to look, knowing that her girl had hooked her up. She hopped out of the chair and Raena immediately plopped herself down in it. "Y'all gone hit the club or something?"

Before either Raena or Shaniqua could respond, Ervin walked in and made a direct line towards them. "Shit!" Shaniqua cursed under her breath. Both Tanya and Raena looked at her, but she ignored their questioning looks. Ervin didn't speak. He grabbed Shaniqua around the waist and planted a sloppy kiss on her lips sucking half of her lipstick off in the process. Shaniqua fought down the bile that rose in her throat.

"Yo, you done? Cool. Let's move, I got shit to do," he said

smacking her on the ass then turning to head back towards the door. Shaniqua had to bite her tongue to keep from cursing his ass out. She gave Raena, then Tanya a quick hug.

"Thanks, girl," she said. "I'll call you later about tonight." She rushed to catch up to Ervin as he opened the door. Once they were outside, her sour mood instantly vanished. Shane was standing in front of her leaning against the brand new Lexus ES.

"What's up?" He said looking at her briefly then looking away. His eyes were like restless orbs. They were looking everywhere but at her again. He opened the back passenger's side door for her.

"Thanks, Shane," Shaniqua said with just a hint of flirtatious seduction. She allowed her fingers to brush his and linger for a moment. Shane looked into her eyes then quickly looked away.

Shaniqua smiled to herself. She saw the simmering lust just below the surface. She made sure that he got an eye full of her ass as she climbed 'into the car. When she looked back, she could see the imprint of his hard dick in the crotch of his jeans.

Turning her attention back to Ervin, she spoke. "So where we going, baby? " At first, Ervin ignored her, then when he felt ready to speak, he did.

"I told you I got some business to handle. I need you and Shane to hold shit down for me. I already told him the scoop. He can fill you in later." He paused then continued. "Imma be out of town fo' a few days."

Because she knew that he expected her too, Shaniqua asked. "Baby, do you want me to roll with you? You know I got yo' back." She leaned forward so that her head was near the front seat. She was talking to Ervin but looking at Shane out of the corner of her eye. Shane stared straight ahead.

"Naw babe. This some shit I got to handle alone. Hell, I ain't even taking Lil' Bro so you know I got to roll solo. But, you handle shit here fo' daddy. I need my baby girl to help hold down the fort."

Shaniqua nodded not believing her luck. Ervin? Gone for a few days? She would be free of him? And, he was leaving her with Shane? It was too good to be true. She immediately suspected a setup. Was Ervin trying to test her?

Trying to see if she would stay down for him? And, was he trying to see if she would try to fuck Shane or another nigga behind his back?

She was still pondering these questions when Shane pulled up in front of the airport entrance, stepped from the car when the two men did. Snatching up his carry-on, the three of them made for the Delta Airlines boarding gate.

Because he had a few moments, Ervin went over a few last minute details with Shane then wrapped his arms around Shaniqua drawing her close.

"Miss me when I'm gone." tie said.

"Always daddy." Shaniqua kissed him in spite of her desire to do otherwise.

Ervin looked deep into her eyes. It was as if he wanted to say something but held back. For the longest moment, they stood wrapped in each other's arms t and locked into each other's gaze.

Finally pulling away, he gave her one more kiss. He briefly

hugged Shane then rushed through the boarding gate. Shaniqua insisted that they remain where they were until the plane was airborne. To an outside observer, she appeared to be reluctant to leave as her lover departed. In actual reality, she was just making sure that his ass actually stayed on the plane.

Back in the car, she turned to Shane, who hadn't/spoken a word. "So, you want to tell me what's going on?" She leaned back on the passenger's side door and stared at him. Shane shifted uncomfortably, cleared his throat, then began to tell her that Ervin was on his way to Vegas.

Ervin was attempting to set up shop in Vegas and needed to see to things personally. Shaniqua listened without interest the minute she realized that the entire thing wasn't a setup. She already knew of Ervin's interest in the sin city. The two of them had spoken about it several times at length.

As Shane spoke, she concentrated on admiring him. Shaniqua kicked off her sandals and pulled her perfectly manicured feet up on the seat and tucked them under her. She saw Shane's eyes follow their movement. He hadn't started the car and they were still sitting at the airport's entrance.

Shaniqua laughed as he jerked his eyes away, and planted them straight ahead. That he had been admiring her smooth thighs was obvious. She had made sure that the dress she wore rode up to reveal them. Shane cleared his throat, started the car and pulled away.

They rode in silence for a while then Shaniqua flipped on the radio. She dialed up her favorite jazz station and leaned back and closed her eyes as the sounds of Paul Hardcastle washed over her.

Jazz music always her always served to take away. She

floated on the melodies and relaxed on the chords. It was like the music became a soothing balm for her tormented soul. It washed over the scars of her life and gave her a sense of peace. When she opened her eyes, she caught Shane staring. He snapped his eyes back on the road. Shaniqua could see the rise in his pants. She reached over and turned down the music. Sade could still be heard softly crooning through the speakers.

"Why do you always do that?" She asked. Shane remained quiet and his eyes stayed straight ahead. "Shane." She said his name softly as if almost in a whisper. Why won't you look at me?"

Shane snapped his light hazel eyes at her then quickly pulled them away. He ran his tongue over his lips and Shaniqua nearly jumped on him right then and there. Still, he didn't speak. She scooted over closer to him and she saw his pulse quicken. "Shane look at me please." She pleaded ever so softly.

That is exactly what Shane did. He looked deep into her eyes. He saw the desire for him written plainly all over her face. He wanted to pull his eyes away from hers, yet she held him captive and she knew it. He watched as she ran her tongue over her sexy lips and he wanted more than anything, to taste them.

He wanted to hold her. To caress her caramel, smooth skin. To taste her juices as they flowed from her body. But, more than anything, he wanted to feel himself buried inside of her moistness.

It took a tremendous amount of effort for him to put his eyes back on the road. His Lust was raw and uncut. He felt the sexual fusion so thickly, the air in the car already smelled as if the two of them had already had sex. He tried to think straight but it was difficult. He knew that Shaniqua thought that he was too shy to talk to her.

Nothing could have been further from the truth. He didn't say much because he knew that if he did, there would be no stopping his desire from being known.

Shaniqua was Ervin's. She belonged to his brother. Shane knew that he couldn't cross that line. In fact, when Ervin had told him of the plan to leave for Vegas and asked him to look after Shaniqua, Shane had done everything in his power to dissuade him.

"Come on 'lil' bro' She ain't that bad. Hell, just keep an eye on her. Make sure she don't get hurt or nothing; That none of these motherfuckers out here disrespect her. Trust me, every-thing will be fine." Ervin had laughed at the look on Shane's face then continued. "Let her and her girls go on a few shop-ping sprees or something. She ain't gone be in the way. Besides, I don't trust nobody but you." With that, he had effectively cut off any more protests.

Shane's mind snapped back to the present when Shaniqua placed her hand lightly on his leg. "Are you gonna answer my question?" She smiled and he almost wrecked the car. Unable to focus, Shane pulled over. Shaniqua was nearly sitting in his lap.

"Damn!" He said. "Shaniqua. Girl...Why are you doing this to me? You know we can't be like this...You and Ervin.." He trailed off as she placed her hand on his chest. "Please Niq...You know we can't do this."

"Do you want me?" She asked softly cutting off Shane's protests. She ran her hand down to his stomach and his felt his muscles clench with desire.

"Do you want me, Shane? If you do, you can have me. You can have all of me." She ran her finger over his hard on and heard him moan. She did it once again. Shane closed his eyes trying hard to shake the grip she had on him. It wasn't working. When he opened them again, her lips were only inches from his. "Kiss me, baby." She whispered. "Kiss me."

Before Shane knew it, their lips were joined. He savored the taste of her feeling it deep down in his soul. He explored her mouth with his tongue while his hands found their way to first her breast, then her thighs. When he ran them up under her dress, he could feel the heat emanating from her throbbing pussy.

Shane knew that he had to have her. Shaniqua pulled back slightly. "Let's go home. I want you Shane. I've always wanted you. Take me and I'll be yours forever."

Shane didn't trust himself to speak. Instead, he pulled back onto the road and made record time getting to his apartment. He wasn't about to go to the place where his brother had made love to Shaniqua. No, he wanted to have her all to himself. He smiled at the thought of finally being able to let his feelings be known and his desire fulfilled.

Within seconds of the door closing, their clothes were off and the two of them were on the floor in the living room entangled in each other's arms. They made wild, unhindered and unbridled love. Shaniqua lost herself in Shane, giving him her all.

Shane eagerly accepted all that she gave, then gave all of himself in return. They climaxed together.

They then moved to the bedroom where they made love the second time. Yet, this time, it was slow and sensual. Shane covered her body with delicate kisses and continuously mumbled her name. "Niq... Oh, Niq."

Shaniqua caressed him and mumbled his name in return. Shane felt her body slake with her second orgasm and moments later, he released himself. Looking into her eyes, he smiled. "I love you Niq. I've always loved you."

"I love you too daddy. I promise you, I will always be yours. I'm yours forever." Shane felt her words in his heart and knew at that moment that he would forever be hers as well. He leaned down and kissed her again.

CHAPTER THREE

The club was packed with hot, sweaty bodies moving and gyrating to the heavy bass music that thumped from the huge speakers. The energized air was thick and filled with the scent of estrogen and testosterone. There was a heavy mixture of cologne, perfume, alcohol, weed, and sex. None of the patrons seemed to mind or find it in any way discomforting, however. Men and women moved through it with delight adding their own little contribution to the mix.

Raena sat at the group's table watching the subtle body language between Shaniqua and Shane. She could tell that there was something different about the two of them. They seemed more relaxed in each other's presence, whereas before, they were always so cold and tense. If she had not known about Shane's fierce loyalty to Ervin, she would swear that they were fucking around.

Speaking of Ervin, Raena wondered for the thousandth time where he was. It wasn't like him no to be out and about. She had tried to ask Shaniqua but her girl was being too evasive.

That in and of itself, was a sign, but a sign of what? Was the two of them having relationship problems? Were they about to do the splits? She could only hope. After all, she wouldn't have a problem with being with Ervin. 'She had always, felt that she was the one who was destined to be with him. Yeah, Shane was fine and all, and she wouldn't have had a problem with letting him hit her pussy up, but it had always been Ervin who really got her juices flowing.

When Ervin had initially gotten with Shaniqua, Raena was more than a little pissed. She couldn't understand it. How could her girl have chosen Shaniqua over her? And, more importantly, how could her girl betray her like that? True, Shaniqua had no idea that she was in love with Ervin, but still, she should have known. After all, that's what friends did. They knew things. Things that didn't have to be said.

Raena knew that she had carried around a grudge against both Shaniqua and Ervin for a long time. Not that either of them noticed, but eventually, she had gotten over it. She had come to grips with the fact that Ervin wasn't hers, probably would never be hers, and Shaniqua was still her girl.

Raena was jarred from her brooding when Tanya dropped down in the seat next to her. "Whew! Girl, it's hot as hell up in here." She fanned herself then took a sip of her bottled water. Tanya noticed Shane and Shaniqua huddle close but didn't pay them any attention. She already had come to the conclusion that the two of them were fucking. In fact, she was surprised that it had taken so long. It wasn't as if nobody knew of the attraction they held for each other, well, anyone who chose to really pay attention. Then again, maybe she could understand why when Ervin was always sweating her.

Turning her attention back to Raena, she continued. "Girl why you ain't got yo' ass out on the dance floor with one of these fine ass niggas?" Raena shook her head. She didn't think Tanya would understand even if she explained.

How could she? After all, no matter how pretty she was, or how nice she dressed, in the end, Tanya was a man. Raena ted never fully accepted the fact that Tanya was a transgendered woman: One who looked, acted, thought and lived completely as a female.

Just because she was born with a male "antenna" didn't change who she was on the inside. Tanya had been taking every last penny she earned and putting it away for her surgery. That it was an expensive procedure was an under-statement. Yet, it was one that she knew was well worth it.

True, there were more than enough other ways to make money, and make it a lot quicker, But, Tanya wasn't one to sell either drugs or her body. She wasn't a dope dealer and she damn sure wasn't a whore.

No. Nor would she allow any man to pay for it. There had been a few who had offered. Tanya had declined them all. This was something she wanted to do herself, and for herself. It was a personal thing that she knew not many people would understand. She was a woman of principles and no matter what the stigma of society was, she refused to compromise them. Likewise, she refused to be labeled and fall into the stereotypical ideology of what most people thought transgenders acted like.

Tanya wasn't wild, whorish, or addicted to drugs or alcohol. She didn't drink, smoke or do any form of drugs. She wasn't promiscuous, she worked a full-time job, and one day planned to own her own shop. She was well educated and had gradu-ated high school at the top of her class. She was well cultured, yet she still had a 'hood flavor to her and had no problem with speaking ebonies or slang. She detested gangs and would never lie caught up in any form of baby mama drama.

"What? You still having man problems?" Tanya asked when Raena didn't answer her the first time. "Girl you need to just settle yo' ass down with a good man. One good man! Then, you wouldn't be moping around all the time."

"I ain't mopping and yo' ass need to mind yo' own damn business." Raena snapped. She sent a hateful glare at Tanya then continued. "Besides, who I fuck ain't nothing you need to lie all up in my damn face about anyway."

"Who the fuck...Bitch, please. That shit ain't no funky ass secret! Hell, everybody knows yo' ass done fucked half the nigga's up in here! Shit, if anything, it's who yo hot ass ain't done fucked." Tanya snapped back. She was fed up with Raena's attitude towards her. She figured that it was about time to put Raena in her place.

"Fuck you, Tanya," Raena shouted. "Yo' ass just mad 'cause don't no real man want to fuck on no dude...." She pushed her drink to the side then continued. Hell, I don t care who much yo gay ass try to dress up and shit, in the end, yo' ass is still a fucking man! 'Fuck on that bitch! "

Before Tanya could even form a reply, Shaniqua jumped in. She knew Tanya was on the verge of kicking Raena's ass. Shaniqua had no desire to see her girls going at each other. "Y'all calm down. Shit! I can't take you bitches no where without y'all showing yo' asses. Raena, you know you wrong! That was foul." She looked at Raena before continuing. "Tanya, girl, leave Raena and who she's fucking out of yo' conversation."

"Whatever Shaniqua," Raena said with an attitude as she snatched up her drink, rose and disappeared into the throng.

Shaniqua shrugged her shoulders, looked at Tanya, then tried to speak. However, before she could, the DJ's voice boomed over the speakers letting everyone know that he was about to slow things down. Teddy Pendergrass's 'Turn out the lights,' immediately followed his words. Shane pulled Shaniqua to her feet and the two of them were followed by several more couples onto the dance floor. Tanya smiled as they hugged each other as only two people who were newly in love could.

Tanya sat admiring all the couples on the floor and wishing for a lover of her on. A real, true lover. She saw several guys approaching her to ask if she cared to dance. She politely turned them down. She didn't feel like being felt up on a dark, crowded dance floor by a completely drunken stranger who swayed from side to side like a wounded ship on the high seas.

Sighing to herself, Tanya leaned back and let the melodic flow of Teddy's voice wash over her as she swayed to the rhythm of the beat. Just as she felt herself overcoming her brief moment of discontent, she sensed someone standing beside her. She looked up with a slight frown on her face prepared to argue with Raene again even though she had no desire to do so.

Her frown instantly changed. Cory smiled down at her. Before she could manage to do more than smile back, he seated himself next to her in Raena's vacated chair.

"Hey boy. I didn't know you was up in here." She said instantly feeling a lightness in her mood. "How long you been here?"

"Long enough to see you sitting here all alone," Cory replied.

"So what is a beautiful woman such as yourself doing sitting here by yourself?" Tanya blushed at the compliment as he continued. "So where's the rest of your click?" He indicated the empty chairs around the table.

"On the floor," Tanya replied. "Raena...Don't know. But, I'm not too concerned about them. They're grown enough to take care of themselves. So what's up with you?" She asked changing the subject.

"Wanting to spend some time with you." He replied flirting. "You think that's possible?"

"Me...." Tanya said obviously surprised. "Urn...Yeah. That's possible." She continued trying to recover from her surprise.

"Good, then can I start by having this dance with you?" He took her by the hand and led her to the dance floor. When he wrapped his arms around her waist, Tanya sent up a silent prayer asking God to let Cory be the one. She felt her prayers answered when she felt Cory's lips press lightly against hers. She offered no resistance as the sweet taste of his tongue brushed hers. Tanya closed her eyes and allowed Cory to take her away.

CHAPTER FOUR

Jessie looked dispassionately at the pleading look on Rock's face, he could care less about granting him the mercy he begged for. Instead, he focused on the desire to inflict serious harm on the man who had seen fit to try and betray him. Who had taken it upon himself to steal from him? And worst of all, Rock had thought he was smart enough to get away with it. That, or he assumed that Jessie was either too dumb to realize what was going on, too lazy or weak or soft to do anything about it if he did know, or too distracted enough to care. Whichever thought spurred his thinking, Jessie was now showing him just how wrong he had been.

Rock now hung from two giant meat hooks that had been pushed through the joints at his shoulder blades. His face had been beaten to a bloody pulp and his naked body shivered from the below temperatures of the freezer they were standing in. The meatpacking plant was just one of several businesses Jessie owned.

Rock stared at Jessie through eyes swollen almost to the point of closure. He desired to speak, yet the smashed teeth and broken jaw prevented him from being able to do so. At best, all he could do was utter a pitiful moan every now and then.

Rock had been the manager of the meat packing plant. He had worked for Jessie for almost five years and although he managed the plant well, his true job had been to oversee the large cocaine smuggling operation Jessie ran out of the place.

Rock and his employees would pack and ship tons of China white Jessie had coming in from numerous sources, in with the frozen slabs of beef and pork, and ship it all over the country.

Rock had one day taken to the notion that with so much drugs coming in and and going out, Jessie would never notice a kilo or two missing from a few shipments a month. He had two of his boys that he knew he could trust, divert the keys, then Rock would sell them and the three of them split the profits.

They had started three years ago with taking only one or two, but as time went on, and greed set in, they grew bolder and bolder until they were taking nearly a quarter of every other shipment. Rock made up for the stolen cocaine by stepping on and stretching the remaining pure shipments. The three of them had each grown quite wealthy due to their side hustle.

Unbeknown to them, Jessie had become aware of the thefts after the very first time, yet he had chosen to remain silent about it. He, instead, watched Rock and his two associates, whose bodies now floated in a thousand pieces in a river somewhere, just to see how bold they would become. And, how many more of workers would join in on the thefts. He was pleased to see that no one else had.

Still, he chose to watch instead of react. Something inside had

told him that there was more going on. He had been right. He
soon learned that Rock was selling the stolen drugs to one of
his enemies. That had almost made Jessie explode yet he
remained calm then went to work on his own plan.

He instructed three of his guys to secretly take the impure
cocaine Rock was sending out in the shipments and switch it
with the pure cocaine he was selling. He then watched and
waited, and sure enough, his enemies started complaining.
Everyone knew Jessie had the best stuff around.

Rock was determined to please his new friend and had
promised to get back on it. He swore to deliver up only the
best. He confronted his two partners thinking that they were
somehow swindling him. Yet, they denied it.

After the confrontation, Jessie instructed his own guys to stop
switching the shipments. Once again, the pure stuff flowed.
Jessie's enemy 'was once again satisfied and Rock was
convinced that his guys had been scheming on him and had
stopped once he had confronted them. Jessie had been
successful at sowing mistrust between Rock and his boys.

Eventually, Jessie's enemy became so pleased with Rock, he
offered him an opportunity Rock was eager to grasp. He
offered Rock the chance to remove Jessie from his throne so
that he could take Jessie's place.

The plan was simple. He wanted Rock to help him in setting
Jessie up to get smoked. Once Rock agreed, Jessie moved in.

The hit was supposed to have gone down earlier when Rock
came to inspect the latest shipment. Of course, when he
arrived, to his surprise, instead of a dead body he was
promised, he found Jessie living and breathing.

When Jessie had his men bind and begin to slowly torture

Rock. He quickly began to confess and plead for his life. Jessie had, of course, simply laughed at him. Instead of the mercy Rock so desperately wanted, Jessie made sure he received intense pain.

Jessie took the gun he held and placed it next to Rock's genitals. "So, you man enough to try and do me hub? Well, shit that means you man enough to die. Stop whimpering like a bitch. Yo' ass is crying like a ho! If you a bitch then you should be used to getting fucked."

Rock looked pleadingly at Jessie but he didn't get the type of response he wanted. "Nigga fuck you!" Jessie shouted. In rapid secession, he pulled the trigger blowing a hole in Rock's nuts then quickly pointed the gun to his head and blew out his brains. Clean this shit up! He told his boys and walked out of the warehouse.

The stretched Mercedes Benz limo was waiting for him and the door was instantly opened by his bodyguard and driver Lucas. Lucas had been by Jessie's side since the day he'd sold his first joint. Jessie thought back to those days as he relaxed in the back, in his seat. He and Lucas both had grown up in the streets. Both of their fathers were street hustlers who had taught them the game from the moment they had taken their first steps. At the same time, Jessie' father Malcolm, was one of only a handful of hustlers who was running his own crew and producing his own products. Lucas' father, Felix, was Malcolm's right-hand man.

Together, the two men had built their little corner hustle into a well-honed organization. When Felix had been killed in a drive-by, Malcolm had taken Lucas and treated him like his own son. Malcolm had died only three years after Felix.

Both Lucas and Jessie had been seventeen, yet Jessie knew

that he was ready to step into his father's shoes. That is exactly what he did. The organization Malcolm had built, Jessie had turned into an empire. He now ran both the entire west and east sides and half of the north.

He instructed Lucas to head to the Top Spot, one of six night-clubs he owned, then had Lucas contact the club's manager. There was one more thing that he needed to take care of.

Closing his eyes, he thought about what his cousin Nadia had told him earlier. She had been pressing him to settle down with a nice girl and relax and enjoy hi's money. She had even suggested that he reunite with the mother of his children, Olivia.

Olivia and Jessie had two children together. Jackson, his son and Aniah, their daughter. Although Jessie loved his children, he could not stand the hood rat mother of theirs. He provided for them, spent time with them, but otherwise, avoided Olivia as much as he could.

No, he wouldn't get back with Olivia, but he would consider settling down with the right woman. The question in his mind was, if she was actually out there, then who was she, and where was she?

CHAPTER FIVE

Shaniqua's week of independence and fun came to a crashing halt the minute Ervin returned. Although she had managed to call him several times between the lovemaking fest she and Shane were having, he immediately pressed her for two things. Details of everything she had done, and sex. Both were, to her, daunting tasks. Somehow she managed to satisfy him with both.

Although her entire being longed to be with Shane, she managed to maintain her composure. The two of them continued to be evasive around each other in Ervin's presence. Even still, they managed to steal quick glances and touches when Ervin was preoccupied. Be that as it may, the change in their once-icy relationship didn't go unnoticed by Ervin. One day, after having made the usual rounds to his cash spots and collecting the money due, he commented on it while the three of them sat around the table in a restaurant eating crabs and lobsters.

Shaniqua was sitting between the men. She was rubbing her

foot up and down Shane's leg under the table and enjoying watching his face as he fought to keep it straight. Ervin asked the question out of nowhere.

"So what's up with you two?" Both Shaniqua and Shane froze. Ervin laughed out loud then continued. "I mean I ain't never seen y'all be so nice to each other before. Hell, just last week Shane was calling you an ice queen."

Shaniqua frowned. "I ain't no damn ice queen!" She shot an angry glare at Shane who was smiling behind a mouthful of food.

"Yeah, you get cold as hell sometimes girl," Ervin replied. He ignored the look she gave him and continued. "I guess a week of having to deal with each other has thawed y'all out some huh?"

Before either she or Shane could comment, Ervin grew serious. As if sensing the shift in his brother's mood, Shane wrapped his hand around the butt of the .45 he held under the table. Shaniqua also saw Ervin's change and instantly became alert.

Her eyes scanned the restaurant and locked on a tall, extremely handsome man who had walked in. He was escorting an exotic and obviously beautiful, sexy woman; He held her arm as they were directed to a table across the room from where she, Ervin and Shane sat.

Suddenly, Ervin rose. "Let's go!" He tossed the napkin down and didn't wait for a reply. Shane and Shaniqua both rose and followed him out. Shaniqua took another look at the striking man at the table and noticed a huge man that she hadn't seen before, standing discreetly a distance away from the couple. Yet, his eyes were not upon them, butcher. She quickly averted her eyes and rushed out after Ervin and Shane.

It wasn't until they were in the Navigator and away from the restaurant that she saw Ervin Visibly relax. She wondered for the hundredth time who the man was. She knew not to ask Ervin, for his temper would instantly flare up. She decided she would find out from Shane as soon as she got the chance.

Ervin whirled on her. "What the fuck you was staring at that nigga fo'." He reached into the back seat and grabbed Shaniqua by the arm. "Hell, you looking at that punk fo' huh?" He shouted.

Shaniqua was so shocked by his actions, she couldn't speak. Ervin had never treated her like this. She instinctively tried to pull back and hi's grip tightened. She stared into his eyes and saw the wild savagery there. Fear gripped her.

"I..I wasn't staring at him." She managed to say.

"Bitch don't lie to me!" He snapped. "I saw yo' ass droolin' after that bitch ass nigga." Before Shaniqua could even register a reply, Ervin smacked her hard across the face. The sound of the blow echoed in the Navigator.

Shane, who was driving, gripped the steering wheel so tight, he thought that it might snap at any moment. He couldn't believe Ervin was putting his hands on Shaniqua. She was his girl! Shaniqua was right, he realized when she had told him that Ervin didn't appreciate or deserve her. She had told him that Ervin was a pig, yet Shane had not wanted to believe her. After all, she was talking about his brother. He now saw that her words were true. He had never seen Ervin acting the was he was. When Ervin slapped Shaniqua a second time, he had to use every ounce of willpower to restrain himself.

"Nigga get yo' fucking hands off me motherfucker!" Shaniqua shouted. She swung hard and connected with the side of

Ervin's head. The blow did little in the way of harm, yet it fueled his rage.

Ervin jumped into the back seat and attacked her with hard blows to her side, arms, legs, and stomach. Shaniqua screamed as she kicked out and lashed out with everything within her. She felt a small sense of satisfaction when her nails raked across his face drawing blood.

"Bitch!" Ervin shouted. He pushed her face into the seat and pounded the back of her head. Shaniqua's screams were muffled by the seat's cushion. "I'm gone kill you bitch! Don't you ever put yo' fucking hands on me!"

With his hands wrapped around her neck, he released all of his pent-up frustrations. All the times he had thought she was cheating on him, all the times he'd seen dudes looking at her with lust in their eyes and hadn't done shit about it, Even all the times he'd had to watch as she admired a nicer car, house or even clothes than she had. All these things had done more to damage his ego, his sense of pride than anyone would ever know.

The way Shaniqua had gawked at the fool in the restaurant had been the final blow. Shit had gone bad in Vegas; worse than he cared to share with Shane and Shaniqua, yet he had chalked it up. His pride was wounded, however. He had designs on pushing into the big league; Of claiming his piece of the pie. He wanted to be able to give Shaniqua whatever she needed at the drop of a dime, yet now, he knew that he couldn't. He couldn't do shit now but lay back and massage his bruised ego.

Seeing her drooling over some other nigga had been too much for him. He knew that Shane had seen her as well. That alone, was more than he knew he could stand. Shane looked up to him. He was his younger brother's shining example. If he couldn't keep his girl's eyes on him, then he knew that Shane would see him as nothing more than just another weak, pathetic ass nigga running around and running off at the mouth. That was something he just couldn't have.

Shaniqua struggled harder against the force of Ervin's body pressing her down. She knew that at any moment, she would suffocate to death. It was already becoming harder for her to breathe and she could no longer hear Ervin's curses or the pleas of Shane's voice. Her survival instincts screamed at her, yet she was no match for the brute strength that held her down.

Suddenly, she found that she was able to breathe. She felt Ervin's weight lifting off of her. She lifted her head and inhaled deeply. The air rushed into her lungs and tasted sweet and refreshing. By the time sound registered back in her dazed mind, Ervin was outside the car engaged in a shouting match with Shane. She climbed from the back seat just in time to see Ervin punch Shane in the face sending him crashing to the ground.

"Punk nigga! Keep yo' fucking hands off me!" Ervin shouted. Cars streamed by them. "Ain't none of yo' business what I do with my bitch! Stay the fuck in yo' place!"

"Fuck you, Ervin! You're a dumb ass nigga!" Shane snapped back. He jumped to his feet and rushed his brother. They collided in a flurry of blows. Ervin hit Shane with two jabs to the face swelling his eye and splitting his lip.

Shane countered with hits of his own. Two to Ervin's ribs and one to the face. He also connected one to the head. Ervin took them in stride and elbowed Shane in the chest. As Shane hit the ground a second time, Shaniqua screamed and launched herself onto Ervin's back.

"Leave him alone nigga!" She raked her nails against his face and the side of his neck. Ervin screamed in rage and flung her off of him. Shaniqua hit the ground hard, knocking the breath out of her.

"Bitch Imma kill you!" He grabbed her by her hair and snatched her to her feet. Before he could punch her, however, Shane cracked him on the side of the head with a discarded beer bottle he'd snatched from the ground. Ervin whirled on his brother. His anger exploded anew. Understanding hit him all of a sudden.

"You fucking her nigga!" He whipped around on Shaniqua, then back to Shane. When neither denied it, his mind became blinded with rage. He punched Shaniqua so hard in the face, he broke her nose. Shaniqua fell to the ground in a shower of blood.

Before Shane could move, Ervin slammed his fist into Shane's chest knocking the wind out of him. "Nigga what the fuck!" He shouted. "You 'spose to be my nigga! You my brother! You gone go behind my back and fuck my bitch? Nigga fuck you!" He hit Shane twice more.

"Yeah, nigga I'm fucking her! I'm fucking her a lot better than you. Yo' bitch ass don't deserve her. Fuck you bitch ass nigga!" Shane shouted back. Ervin swung on him yet this time, Shane anticipated it. He dodged the swing and punched Ervin hard in the face twice, then twice more.

Ervin stumbled back. Before he thought about what he was doing, Shane wrapped his hands around the butt of the gun he still had tucked in the waistband of his pants. He pulled it out. He pointed it squarely at Ervin's chest.

"What! Nigga you gone shoot me? I'm yo' fucking brother! You gone kill me cause I kicked yo' ass? You pointing that thang like it makes you a man."

Shane didn't speak. His eyes were hard. In his mind, all he could see was Shaniqua on the ground bloody. All he had to do was turn his head slightly to confirm the vision in his mind. He could hear her moaning in pain.

"Bitch? Naw bro, you're the whose a bitch. You the one acting like a ho'. Yo' punk ass is hitting on a woman. What? That make you feel like a man? You ain't no man. You're a bitch! Yo punk ass can't even satisfy a real woman like Niq!" Shane shook with rage. All of his anger, all of his frustrations with Ervin boiled to the surface.

Shane suddenly saw Ervin in a new light. He saw that Shaniqua was right. He had been standing for too long in Ervin's shadow. It was past time for him to step up and start making moves on his own. "Naw, you ain't no man. I don't know why I ain't never seen it before. You're a real bitch and ain't got no heart."

Before Ervin could speak, Shane pulled the trigger twice, sending two slugs into Ervin's chest. Ervin staggered back a step then dropped to the ground. Shane turned from his dead brother's body and helped Shaniqua to her feet.

As she wiped the blood from her face, the cloth she held hid her smile. Shane held her briefly before turning to pull Ervin's corpse off the road and into the ditch on the side. By the time they left the scene, the body had begun to grow cold.

CHAPTER SIX

Raena was shocked at the news she had gotten from her boyfriend, Dejuan. The two of them had been out at the mall. Dejuan was doing what he usually did when he was trying to apologize to her for some shit he had done. With an arm full of bags filled with designer clothes and shoes, he was running off at the mouth about any and everything. "That nigga got capped and dumped on the side of the road. That's what his bitch ass get. His punk ass brother needs to get popped too."

"Who you talking about?" Reana asked. "Who got killed?" She stopped to look at Dejuan causing him to stop 3S well. "Who you talking about?" She asked again.

"That punk ass nigga Ervin. They found his ass like two days ago. Somebody peeled his cap." Dejuan didn't notice the look of horror on Raena's face. He continued to yap as they started back walking.

Raena was lost in thought. Ervin? Dead? It couldn't be true.

How? Who killed him? Suddenly, she thought about Shaniqua. It had been two weeks since the two of them had mixed words over Tanya. She had been pissed that Shaniqua kept defending Tanya and had decided that she would just back away from the two of them for a while. But still, the news of Ervin's death changed all that. After all, Shaniqua was still her girl. Surely she must be devastated.

Whipping out her phone, she dialed Shaniqua's number. When it was picked up on the third ring, Raena was shocked not to hear her girl's voice but that of a man. "Uh...Hello. May I speak with Shaniqua please?" The voice sounded vaguely familiar to her.

"She's in the shower right now. Can I take a message?"

"Uh...Sure. Would you tell her that Raena called and to please call me. as soon as she can?"

"Raena? What's going on girl?...It's Shane." Shane said after she didn't recognize his voice. "Hold on. Let me go get Niq."

Before Raena could respond, she heard a click as the phone was being placed down. A few moments later, it was picked back up and Shaniqua's voice came through the speakers. "Raena? Girl, what's up?"

Raena was slightly taken aback by the cheerful sound of Shaniqua's voice. She had expected to find her in a state of mourning. In fact, as she thought about it, Shane didn't sound too sorrowful either. From what she could detect, Shaniqua did not have a hint of sorrow. "Hey, Shaniqua. Are you okay?"

"Yeah girl, I'm fine." Shaniqua laughed. "What's good with you?"

"Well girl, I just wanted to check on you and make sure that you were alright. I just heard about Ervin. I'm sorry." Raena said.

Shaniqua's voice suddenly took on a new tone. "Yeah girl, that was some messed up shit. It's some foul ass niggas out there in the world. Shaniqua proceeded to tell Raena the fake story that she and Shane had concocted.

Raena couldn't believe it. Apparently, Ervin had been kidnapped for ransom and killed when Shane was unable to provide the kidnappers with the million dollars that they were demanding.

Once Shaniqua finished, Raena remained silent for quite a long time. She felt in her heart that something wasn't right. The story Shaniqua told sounded too rehearsed. Yet, she kept her doubts to herself. When she hung up, she started to relay her doubts to Dejuan but something compelled her to keep her mouth shut. She spent the rest of the shopping spree sad for the loss of the man she loved.

CHAPTER SEVEN

Cory held Tanya close and inhaled the scent of her perfume. She smelled of roses. Ha smiled to himself. Who would have ever believed that he would be so happy? Or, that he could have found a love so powerful in the arms of a transgendered woman? Him? The man who used to look down with disdain on anyone who he even considered weak or a sissy.

He had grown up in an environment that demanded that a man be hard, emotionless, brave, macho and sometimes ruthless. An environment that was quick to pounce upon any perceived weakness or flaw. He had held the belief that anyone who was gay, or transgendered were prey to more powerful people.

Once he had realized that he had started developing feelings for Tanya, he had nearly had a heart attack. How? He wasn't gay! He knew that she was transgender, yet in truth, he had no real clue as to what that really meant. He thought that she was just a pretty guy who wanted to dress up like a woman.

For weeks he was at war with his feelings. He wasn't gay! He had no desire to be with a man. He loved pussy and always would love pussy. He found himself stressing out about his feelings so much that he didn't want to eat. He'd lost his appetite.

Because of the war with himself, he decided that he would no longer go into the shop to get his hair done by her. Yet each time, he found himself making his way to the shop and in truth, to her. He found that he was always eager to see her. And, when he did, he found that the person he saw was a beautiful woman. Not a man.

Her voice, her smell, her looks, everything about her was uniquely feminine. She was both graceful and classy. Yet, she also had a swagger about her that any hood chick would envy. And even still, she wasn't ghetto.

The night at the club when he had seen her, something had come over him and he found that he couldn't stand the thought of not being with her, or at least telling her how he was feeling. When he'd asked her to dance, he had never been more nervous in 'his life. Yet, he was determined to ask. When she said yes and she was in his arms, Cory found that for the first time in his life, he felt complete.

As the weeks went by, he found that he not only felt complete, but truly loved for the first time. Before Tanya, every other woman he'd been width or even though he loved, had been superficial. On the surface, things always seemed to be good, yet deep down inside, he knew that what he was feeling was not that soul stirring connection he longed for.

Tanya stirred his soul and more. She made him feel like he was living a dream. She was so attentive to him, yet she was by far art independent woman. She wasn't clingy or needy. She was attentive because she truly wanted to be, simply-because-it was what she wanted. She gave him a sense of acceptance.

Even still, she was fiercely protective of him, but not in a jealous sense. She had laughed when one day, the two of them were at the grocery store and they had run into one of his ex's. After the girl finished flirting with him and basically trying and failing to intimidate her, Tanya told him that she knew he was beautiful and that all women were attracted to that beauty.

"Baby let them lust. I don't care. All I care about is me having your heart and you having mine." She told him.

Besides opening his eyes to the wonders of true love, Tanya had also enlightened his mind to the true meaning of being transgender. She had, in essence, shown him that she was wholly and indeed a woman. Her physical makeup was irrelevant and would soon be corrected.

Likewise, she had shown him that everyone, no matter their sexual preference, race, gender, religion or nationality, was to be respected. "In truth babe, there is really only one race and that's the human race." She had told him. "We all in a sense, want the same things in life. We all want to be loved. We all want to be happy. We all want to feel safe and secure; to provide for ourselves and our families. To have food to eat, shelter over our heads and clothes on our backs. Why should we spend our time hating someone who only wants the same things in life that we do?"

Cory watched as Tanya rolled over onto her side and continued to sleep soundly. Her chocolate skin glowed in the dim light that shone in the bathroom and spilled over into the darkened bedroom. He smiled and ran his hands lightly over the curve of her hip and butt.

Just like his mind, Tanya had illuminated him sexually. The first time they had gone at it, he had 'been afraid, not knowing what to expect. After all, even though she was without a doubt completely feminine, she did still have a male sex organ and would continue to do so until her surgery.

Tanya however, soothed his fears and assured him that she had no desire and would not in any way, be a challenge or threat to his manhood. In fact, she • assured him that due to the hormone treatment she was undergoing, that part of her anatomy did not even function. Once she calmed his fears, she proceeded to give him the best sex he had ever experienced.

Tanya, Cory found, was: not only a very outspoken woman, but one who possessed a keen intellect. She knew so many things and always seemed to have a thirst foreknowledge. She read relentlessly and was even taking online college courses. She was also, he had learned, a serious health fanatic. Stile worked out each morning and ate healthy meals.

Cory found out that she was an excellent cook. There were not too many things she couldn't fix. She was also a nature lover who constantly preached to him of the necessity of being a conservationist. "After all, this earth is the only home we have, and we have to take care of it."

As he lay watching her, Cory realized that there wasn't a single thing about Tanya he didn't like. Even when he had finally admitted to her what he did for a living, she didn't balk at it. Instead, she asked him to show her the ropes and to teach her how to not only shoot a gun, but how to care for them also.

To his surprise, and her delight, she had turned out to be a pretty good shooter, and with a little patience and practice, would grow into a formidable marksman. It wasn't long before she started accompanying him whenever he went to make a sale.

Tanya quickly became the woman of his dreams. True, he had received scorn from many of his ex-girlfriends and had heard the whispers and taunts a lot of his so-called homies threw at him behind his back. They called him a punk, fag and all the other derogatory terms, yet he knew that not a single one of them would ever say it to his face. Besides, instead of growing angry like he would have done in the past, he now simply shrugged off the intended insults and kept on moving.

It was like Tanya had told him, the ones that always Had something negative to say were the ones who were usually insecure about themselves and hid that in- secure ty behind taunts and bullying tactics. "As long as your happy and secure in who you are babe, fuck those who hate." She had told him.

The one person who surprised Cory and stood by his side and stuck up for him was Lance Bailey. Lance had been shocked upon seeing Cory and Tanya together, yet not in the sense of disgust. No, he was shocked because just like Cory and a lot of other guys, he too had a thing for her. Tanya represented something erotic and forbidden. She was sexy and sensual, and she was considered taboo in the circle with which he ran. There had been many nights when Lance had thought about approaching her yet had never worked up the courage to do so.

Cory and Lance began to hang out together. Before, they had only associated with each other on occasion. Tanya was well aware of Lance's affection for her yet she kept it to herself. After, all, she was more than happy with Cory, had no interest in Lance and did not see a need to cause a rift between the two of them. Plus, it wasn't like Lance had made any advances at her. When and if he did, she was sure that she would deal with it. She had vowed that nothing would come between the happiness that the two of them shared.

CHAPTER EIGHT

Shane moved with a confident stride with Shaniqua by his side. He moved through the crowd that had gathered at the front of the club. After giving the bouncer at the door a pound, he took Shaniqua by the hand and led her inside. The place was packed. The music was loud and the crowd was energized. Shane led her directly to the V.I.P. section where they quickly settled at a table and the waitress brought over an unopened bottle of Crystal. Shaniqua filled two glasses and handed one over to him. As he sipped his drink, he allowed his eyes to scan the crowd.

Shaniqua knew that she was the envy of every woman around. She was dressed to impress in a pair of form-fitting black leather pants, a tight white blouse, and six-inch stiletto boots. Her hair and make-up were flawless and she relished the attention she received from all the men that laid eyes upon her. Although she was enjoying it, however, she did not let it show. She was focused on the task at hand.

Shane absently rubbed her hand. Several women tried to

catch his eye, but he ignored them. Many of the guys, he knew. He and- Ervin had done business with quite a few of them. They acknowledged him with a nod of their heads and he acknowledged them in turn. Even still, none were the man he was looking for.

Even though he wasn't in the crowd, Shane wasn't worried. He leaned back and relaxed with his drink. As ha sipped, he allowed the alcohol to soothe his tension.

They spent over forty minutes at the V.I.P. Shaniqua excused herself and made her way to the dance floor where she proceeded to shake her groove thang until she was drenched in sweat and the guy sire had been dancing with: had an agonizing hard on from the tantalizing dance she had done.

Shane never left his seat. He held a small talk with a few of the guys who'd briefly stopped, making promises to handle business with him in the future. When Shaniqua made her way back to the table, Shane noticed the person he'd been waiting for making his way towards them.

Valentino Nadi was a tall, slender, yet well-built man of both Indian and Spanish descent. He was twenty-seven, six-three and possessed both a sharp mind and an insatiable appetite for all things erotic and exotic. His father and older brothers ran the most lucrative and expansive cartel in the entire city.

His mother, Sanni, was originally from India and his father, Alejandro, was from Spain. Both came from wealthy families that had earned their wealth via trades on the black market. Alejandro's family dealt in stolen paintings and rare artifacts while Sanni's family dealt in human trafficking.

Valentino's older brother, Raphel, was Don of the western branch of the family's empire and held down the entire coast. His brother Luciano was Cappa of the Felitino branch of the family and operated mainly across the U.S. borders, both the Canadian and Mexican, yet his central location was in Detroit.

Valentino had been sent to establish this branch of the family and Shane Wilcox was to be his first contact. Word was that Shane was well connected and reliable to a fault. Valentino had asked his father why they didn't just move into the city and take over, which he would have had no qualms about doing, yet his father had insisted that he wanted no bloodshed or as little as possible. He also explained to his eager son that by establishing solid contacts and creating a good business relationship, Valentino would not only avoid bloodshed and the intense scrutiny of the law that would surely come, he would also gain an advantage over his rivals for he would already have a hand in with the locals.

Shane rose and greeted Valentino with a firm handshake. The two men sized each other up. This was their first face to face meeting, but both had spoken over the phone several times, They both had also done their homework as well. Valentino knew that Shane had recently suffered the loss of his older brother Ervin. He immediately offered his condolences. Shane nodded then turned and introduced Shaniqua. When she took Valentino's hand, she felt him caress her palm with his fingers as his dark eyes ran over her body. When he smiled at her, she held no doubt about what it promised. She smiled her promise back in return.

Turning back to Shane, Valentino took his time discussing the extent of the business he wanted to partner. It was true that he and his family had their own products and their own network to bring it in, what they didn't have, however, was the inside connects to the hood, the barrios, and the ghettos. For that, he needed Shane to run his operation. In return, he assured Shane that his rewards would exceed even his wildest expectations.

Shane listened without making many comments. Everything Valentino said sounded good. Almost too good in fact. He knew he had to move with caution. Plus, he had no desire to give up his spot as top dog of his own crew only to become a lap dog by working for someone else. As Valentino spoke, Shane scanned the people in the club closer. He noticed several men watching them intently, while at the same time, pretending that they were not. Shane knew instantly that they were Valentino's men.

The two of them spoke for twenty more minutes. All the while, Shaniqua kept her eyes on Valentino. She was captivated by him. Valentino was well aware of her thoughts, yet remained nonchalant about it. He knew that Shaniqua was Shanes and had no desire to create a hostile relationship over a woman. Still, something about her stirred his fetish. He found himself wanting to know her. He ended their meeting with an offer for Shane and Shaniqua to dine with him. Shane accepted and stood. After shaking Shane's hand and lightly brushing his lips across the palm of Shaniqua's, Valentino departed. Moments later, his four bodyguards followed.

Shane, feeling good about the way the meeting had gone, popped a bottle of Crystal and he and Shaniqua toasted their success. Just as they were beginning to relax, they were interrupted by the sound of someone speaking to Shaniqua. She looked up and saw Jovan, the guy she had danced with earlier. "Hey ma, can a brother get that dance you promised me?" He looked past Shane as if he didn't exist. Shaniqua was appalled at Jovan's audacity. Before she could utter a reply, Shane stood.

"She's with me, bro. Ain't gone be no more dancing!" He positioned himself in front of Jovan. "I suggest you go find someone else."

"I ain't ask you, nigga. I'm talking to her," Jovan snapped, "If she..." He didn't get the chance to finish. Shane had reached back and hit him with a two-piece short jab that sent him hard to the floor.

"Damn, he put that nigga on his pockets." Someone in the crowd shouted. Jovan shook his head and stumbled to his feet. He tried to refocus on Shane but was seeing double. When he did manage to focus, Shane had Shaniqua by the hand and was walking past. Jovan rushed him. Before he could get close, however, Shane whirled around and pointed his gun in Jovan's face. Jovan froze.

"Nigga, you better think twice," Shane said, his voice was a deadly calm. Jovan eyed the gun, then Shane. He slowly began to back away. Shane watched him until he was a safe distance away, then continued towards the exit. Just as they reached the door, he whipped around and smacked Jovan, who had tried to snake him, in the face.

The crack of Jovan's jaw breaking was heard even over the pounding of the music. Jovan screamed as he fell to the floor. Shane ignored it. He stepped over Jovan and pointed the gun down at him. He wanted to knock the fool's noodles right then and there, yet Shaniqua restrained him. Shane reluctantly allowed her to lead him away and out of the club.

CHAPTER NINE

Jessie Lay impassively next to Sylvia's sleeping form. He watched with disinterested eyes as she curled closer to him in an effort to reap the-bedsits of the warmth his body gave off. The two of them had been "seeing" each other for nearly a year and a half, and although Sylvia expressed a great degree of interest in him, Jessie, for his part, felt nothing.

Oh, Sylvia was indeed, a remarkable and beautiful woman, one whom any man would be proud to have as his own. Any man, that is, save himself. No matter how he tried, Jessie could not seem to feel the love that most people claimed. It eluded him and had done so his entire life. He, at one point, had come to the conclusion that love was just another myth to be placed in the same category as the tooth fairy or santa clause or any other childhood fantasy. Instead of wasting his time chasing after an illusion, he devoted his energy to building his empire and ruling it with an iron-clad fist.

Sex, for him, had nothing to do with love. It was simply another necessity of life, one that he most often, could do without. On those occasions when his desire for sex became too great to ignore, Sylvia provided him the relief he needed. Her sexual prowess was indeed quite satisfying. It was more for that reason alone, he had remained with her for as long as he had. Yet still, he found that she was becoming a bore. She held nothing of interest for him.

Involuntarily, his mind shifted back to Olivia. He had once believed that he was in love with her. He had found himself catering to her every whim. He'd lavished her with gifts, took her on expensive trips and provided her with a plush home and exotic cars. That, of course, had been when he was as naive and as green as any teenage boy freshly entering puberty would be.

The first time he'd laid eyes on Olivia, he'd thought she was a vision of paradise. She was smart, sassy and sexy. When she had smiled at him, she'd taken his breath away. When he'd introduced himself to her, she simply said, "I know." Her confidence had him spellbound. It wasn't long before their casual acquaintance moved towards what Jessie thought was romance. When they turned sixteen, Olivia announced that she was pregnant. Jessie had been ecstatic. He, with the help of his father, purchased a nice home for Olivia, himself and their soon to be son.

Olivia had been excited about the home and the many expensive gifts Jessie and Malcolm lavished her with. The joy one would have assumed she had at the birth of her son, was non-existent. Olivia had long ago, come to the conclusion that her son was simply a means to keep her connected to Jessie should the two of them ever part ways. She, however, never let her feelings about the matter show. Instead, she played the role of a doting mother and a faithful woman to her man. In truth, she was having a secret affair with one of the bodyguards Malcolm had assigned to her. Jessie was as clueless as everyone else, of her infidelity.

A year after the birth of Jackson, Olivia became pregnant again. When Aniah was born, Jessie couldn't have been happier. Her birth came just months after the loss of his father Malcolm, and him having taken over the family business. Olivia held no more joy over the birth of her daughter than she had of that of her son. Her view about children never changed. They were and always would be nothing more than the means to the end that kept her connected to the wealth and power that Jessie wielded.

It wasn't until Jessie had turned nineteen that he became aware of Olivia's cheating and then only by accident. The bodyguard, Marcus, had been caught trying to swipe two keys of black tar heroin from a stash spot Jessie had. When Jessie was informed, he commenced torturing Marcus.

Marcus, when he knew he was about to die, pleaded for both mercy and his life. In the process, confessed to having been not only sleeping with Olivia but stealing the drugs for her. He admitted to having a drug problem and also confessed that she had one as well. Jessie was so livid, he had Marcus' body flayed and tossed into the river.

Rushing home, he burst into their bedroom startling Olivia and catching her on her knees with her head shoved between the thighs of the nanny they'd hired to help with the kids, eating her pussy. Both women were shocked and scared, neither could utter a word. Jessie was disgusted. The nanny, Ms. Polly, was an elderly woman of sixty-four and weighed over two hundred pounds. She always smelled of mothballs and prunes. She spoke with an unfamiliar accent that Jessie always found uncomfortable.

"You nasty bitch!" Jessie shouted. He was repulsed by the sight. He advanced into the room as the two women scrambled around trying to find their clothing. Ms. Polly kept her eyes downcast and Olivia stuttered as her mind worked feverishly trying to come up with something to say. Jessie didn't give her a chance.

Drawing his gun, he pointed it at the nanny. "Get out bitch. Now!" He screamed and cocked the hammer when she hadn't moved. Ms. Polly abandoned all attempts at salvaging her clothes and bolted naked through the door. Jessie didn't spare her another glance.

Grabbing Olivia by the throat, he slammed her to the ground and shoved the barrel of the gun in her mouth. Olivia's eyes grew wide as she stared up into the face of death. Jessie gritted his teeth against the pain of her betrayal.

His hand trembled as she fought within himself. Part of him wanted to blow her brains out; to make her suffer; to hurt just as he was. Her betrayal had cut deeper than she would ever know.

The other part immediately thought of his children. They were his precious jewels. He loved them more than anything in the world. Although Olivia's scandalous ways pained him more and more with each passing second, the thought of his babies growing up without her, hurt him even more. He didn't want them to suffer because of what she had done and his reaction to it.

Reluctantly, he withdrew the pistol's barrel coated with saliva, from her mouth and snatched her to her feet by her hair. Her eyes darted around the room for a possible safe haven or means of escape. As if reading her mind, Jessie backed away. "Don't ever speak to me again bitch. If you do,

Imma kill you. I want nothing else to do with you." He turned and stormed back out of the house. Since that day, almost eight years ago, he and Olivia rarely spoke two words. He provided for his kids and that was all.

Jessie was pulled back to the present as Sylvia turned on her side and pulled the comforter tighter around her naked and bared shoulders. Her light snoring never broke rhythm as she continued to sleep. Jessie rose from the bed, his naked body glistened in the moonlight that shown through the penthouse windows.

He moved with ease over to it and stared out at the city stretched out, beyond the panes. Yes, Sylvia was a wonderful woman, yet Jessie knew that she was not the one for him. He had grown bored with her presence and decided to cut her loose in the morning. He needed to refocus his energy on the running of his organization. He knew that there was a new player in town, some guy from out of Chicago, who was starting to make waves. If word on the streets was true, this guy was quickly snapping up all the small time hustlers and uniting them into one force. A force that was by no means, as formidable as his own, but one never the less. He knew this guy bore watching.

Jessie didn't really care about those nickel and dime hustlers, for none of them worked for or had any dealing with him. They operated on the north side and didn't infringe upon his territory. As long as things remained that way, he would leave things be. After all, there was more than enough meat on the table for everyone to eat. He wasn't greedy. But, he was, he knew, a hungry man.

CHAPTER TEN

Tanya pulled up to the Slow Cook Bar and Grill in her brand new Porsche Boxter with the top down. The fifty-seven-thousand-dollar car was metallic silver with silver and white interior. Cory had purchased it for her and had surprised her with it for her twenty-fifth birthday. She smiled to herself as she stepped out dressed in a pair of tiger print, form fitting, jeans that were caressing every curve of her body. She wore a pair of four-inch heels, a tan blouse and a tiger print scarf that held her flowing auburn colored hair back. A pair of diamond earrings sparkled in her ears and matched the diamond bracelet that wrapped around her slender wrist. The diamond ladies supreme edition Rolex watch also caught its share of the sun's rays.

Making her way inside, she removed the pair of two-hundred-dollar Louie Vuitton stunner shades that covered her eyes and placed them inside the oversized Louie Vuitton handbag that was strapped over her shoulder. Scanning the slightly dim lit interior, she spotted both Shaniqua and Raena sitting at one of the booths near the back and quickly made her way over. Her girls smiled as she dropped into the cushioned seat next to Raena.

They both had baskets of spicy flavored buffalo wings in front of them and from the pile of bones laying next to the baskets, had been busy knocking a dent into them. They had bottles of Corona beer at their sides. She quickly stopped a passing waitress and ordered her own basket and beer. "Damn girl, it's hot as hell out there." She complained.

"Not as hot as that outfit yo' ass is wearing," Shaniqua replied. "Where you get it?" She sucked on a bone then took a swallow of beer.

"Mervyn's girl. They got all kinds of stuff on sale right now." Tanya turned to Raena. "What's wrong girl? Why you so quiet?" She and Raena had made up, yet Tanya could still sense a little tension between the two of them. She tried her best to squash it. After all, Raena was her girl and all three of them had grown up together.

Raena shrugged her shoulder and continued to eat her wings. Tanya's inquiry was interrupted when the waitress returned with her order. She quickly dove into her basket and beer. All conversation between them ceased as they ate. All that is, except when they stopped their waitress to order more beer.

After the wings, they sat catching each other up on what had been going on with them. Since the last time they had all hung out together, Shaniqua told them about the new condo on the south side that Shane had purchased for them and the new Infiniti he'd gotten her. Tanya had noticed the car as she'd pulled up to the place.

She, in turn, told them of the Porsche Gory had purchased for her and that she was now living with him. The two of them was going strong and Cory was falling more in love with her each day. She, at just the thought of him, found herself feeling flushed. It was as if his presence was right there with her.

Of the three of them, Raena's life was the only one that seemed to be stuck in a rut. She still lived in the same projects she had been living in and drove the same old beat up Toyota Camry that she'd had for the past three years. De- Juan, her current ex-boyfriend, had promised to move her out of the ghetto and buy her a new ride. That promise had never been fulfilled.

About three weeks ago, Raena had caught him on the phone having phone sex with some unknown female. He had closed himself in the closet late one night when he had thought she was sleeping. In fact, she had been until the absence of his presence in bed beside her had woken her. When she had gone searching for him, she heard his voice coming from the hallway closet. Snatching open the door, she found him hunched over with the phone to his ear, his pants down and his dick in his hand jacking off. He had been so startled to see her, he spilled semen all over her broom and dustpan.

Raena had been so furious, she'd kicked him out right then and there. She learned later that he had been staying four apartments down with a neighbor named Vera. Vera was thirty-seven, had five kids by four different men and survived solely off the support she received from the county. Well, that and the occasional trick she turned. The two of them held a casual acquaintance. Although they were not enemies, neither were they friends. They only spoke to say hi or bye to each other when they saw, one another.

For three weeks, DeJuan had stayed away. Raena admitted to herself that she was lonely and missed him. He'd shown up to her door two days ago begging her to take him back. She had turned him away but had said that she would consider it if he promised to change his ways. Of course, he promised.

The next morning, she received a visit from Vera. After Raena invited her in and offered something to drink, Vera proceeded to tell her that DeJuan had been living with her and the two of them had been having sex. In fact, they had been going at it with each other for the past six months. DeJuan had been paying her for sex and had, in fact, become one of her favorite customers. She even confessed to Raena that she was the woman DeJuan had been having phone sex with.

Raena sat in silence as Vera poured the story out. Once she was done, Raena asked, "Why are you telling me all this now? After all, like you just said, y'all been fucking behind my back for six months."

Vera put her head down and tears welled up in her eyes. She looked back up and Raena could see the sorrow in her face. "Two days ago, I found out that I'm HIV positive. I'm sick." The tears spilled down her cheeks. "I don't know who I got it from or how long I've had it, but I got it now. I... You need to go get yo' self-checked out. I told DeJuan about it and he just walked out and left me." Vera stood and moved towards the door. "I gotta go get my kids checked cause they might have it too." With that, she opened the door and left.

Raena remained sitting in her chair staring at the door, too stunned to move. HIV? She couldn't have HIV. She could get AIDS and die, and all because of DeJuan's bitch ass. That nigga had been cheating on her all this time! She found her own tears stinging her eyes and absently wiped them from her face.

He had been cheating on her with a woman who had AIDS and after finding out had left and tried to come crawling back! Raena felt an anger building in her like a flood. She suddenly rose from her seat and went to the kitchen. She snatched up her large butcher's knife, wrapped her hand around the handle and sat back down to wait. She knew DeJuan would show up at her door sooner or later.

She was right. Around eight in the evening, he knocked on the door. Raena rose and went to open it. As she did, DeJuan stood there with a dozen red roses, He started to speak but quickly forgot his words as Raena slashed at him with the knife. "You nasty son of a bitch!" She shouted slashing at him a second time. "Imma kill you motherfucka!"

As DeJuan dodged the knife, he dropped the flowers and backed away. Raena followed in hot pursuit. "You cheating motherfucka! You AIDS having bitch! Imma kill you!"

It didn't take but a split second for DeJuan to figure out what had happened. He didn't get the chance to explain nor did he try. He turned and bolted out of the apartment complex, moving as fast as he could. Raena gave chase, but was no match for his speed. As he disappeared from sight, she returned to her place where she bolted herself in, fell in her bed and cried herself to sleep.

Raena suddenly looked up. "I think I got AIDS." She blurted out. Both Tanya and Shaniqua instantly grew quiet. The buffalo wing Shaniqua was sucking on, dropped from her fingers and fell to the floor. Tanya sat the beer down and swallowed hard. Neither of them knew what to say. Raena didn't give them a chance. She rushed into her story and told them what had happened. Tears spilled from her face as she spoke and soon both Tanya and Shaniqua were crying as well. When she finished, they all sat in silence for a while.

"Well, I'll go with you to the clinic." Tanya offered. Shaniqua offered her support as well. Raena nodded. In spite of it all, it felt good knowing that her girls had her back.

CHAPTER ELEVEN

The clinic was both loud and packed. As Tanya led the way in, Shaniqua moved through the doors and Raena slowly brought up the rear a bit more reluctantly. Looking around, Tanya spotted three chairs and Shaniqua led Raena over. Tanya however, moved to the counter and spoke with the duty nurse. Moments later, she returned with a clipboard, pen and both a medical and consent form. She handed them to Raena.

Raena had spent the night with both Shaniqua and Tanya. They had stayed at her place. Neither was too sure of Raena's mental state and didn't want to leave her alone. She looked at the forms with blurry eyes and without speaking, began to fill them out. Neither Shaniqua nor Tanya spoke yet both lent their girl strength. All three looked over at the counter as the voices of a group of women rose.

The four women varied in age. The eldest was a scrawny dark-skinned woman with grey hair and a harsh looking face. Two of the women looked to be the same age; in their mid to late thirties. The fourth was a young girl who couldn't have been more than fifteen. The three older women were doing most of the talking and were obviously speaking at times, to or about the young girl.

"I told yo' ass way too many damn times ta' leave that no-good ass boy alone. But no. You just had ta' have him. Talkin' 'bout 'mama he's so fine,' an all that shit. Now, look at ya ass!" One of the women in her thirties said. She was slightly plump and had more ass and tits than she knew what to do with.

"Ummm Hmmmmm!" The other lady beside her said. "You right 'bout that Val. See, that's what the fuck I mean, you have to watch out fo' niggas like that. They don't care. They be havin' all kinds of diseases and shit. They just brush it off and pass that shit on to every woman stupid enough to lay down and cock they legs open for them."

Val laughed and nodded. Both the elderly woman and the young girl remained quiet. The young girl with her head down. "Damn right. Remember the down low? A lot of these niggas be just like that. Well, we got to learn to get down low too. Only thing is, we gotta get down low and investigate these nigga's dick heads." Both she and the other woman speaking laughed.

"Shit, girl, you gotta get down low, grab a magnifying glass and a pair of tweezers and act like yo' ass is Inspector Gadget or something. Like yo' ass is Dora the Explorer and be on the hunt like where the hell is Waldo. Fo' real. You know you can't be trusting these gutta ass niggas. They quick to give a bitch crabs or something. And, I ain't talkin' 'bout no seafood neither. This ain't no Captain's or Red Lobster." The two women laughed even louder.

"It ain't even like that mama. Rodney's not like that. He loves me and I love him." The young girl cried clutching her hands tightly around her body.

"Girl please," Val said to her daughter. "You hear her dumb ass, Tiffany?" She asked the other woman. Tiffany nodded and continued to laugh. "Don't no man love a woman girl! They just tell yo' ass that shit ta get what they want. The only thang they love is getting their dick wet. Get ya damn head out the clouds. This ain't no la-la land, in case yo' ass ain't noticed." She waved her hand to indicate the clinic's waiting room. "This is what a man's so-called love gets you. Yo' ass is the one sittin' here burnin' with the damn claps."

"Let it be Val. Leave the child alone." The older woman spoke. Her voice was the lowest of them all yet the weight of what she said could be felt through her mother. Why don't you try comforting her instead of beating her down with your words!"

Raena, although she said nothing, sympathized and related to the young girl. She caught the girl's eye and smiled her reassurance. The girl gave a weak smile back. The elderly woman gave the gesture and nodded to Raena.

After finishing her forms, Raena took them to the nurse then returned to her seat. A few minutes later, the nurse came, gathered up the young girl and ushered her in back to one of the examination rooms. The elderly woman accompanied her. The two other women ignored them and continued to speak on their plans for their night out at the club. Raena sat in silence, awaiting her turn.

CHAPTER TWELVE

Shaniqua was still a little shaken by Raena's episode. It would take about a week to get the results. She curled on the sofa with her feet tucked under her telling Shane what had happened. Shane listened impassively. He really didn't care one way of the other. His mind was preoccupied with dealing with Valentino. The two of them had been sharing the profits of their partnership, yet Shane could see the scheme that Valentino was plotting. He'd watched as Valentino had taken over the small crews that operated in the lower north side. Shane had adamantly refused to turn over control of his own crew, even while he managed Valentino's operation. He was determined to keep his own product and profits separate from his partners.

"Babe, we gotta make some moves." Shane suddenly said, cutting off Shaniqua's story. "We got to plan some shit. This nigga Valentino is getting a little too greedy. The nigga is snapping up shit way too fast and nigga's out in them streets ain't feelin' this shit." He rose and stepped over to the bar and poured himself a drink. He didn't return to the sofa, however. Instead, he moved into a spare room. Shaniqua quickly followed. When she saw Shane go to the safe and start stacking piles of money onto the bed, she knew that shit was getting real serious.

"What's that for baby?" She asked. She sat on the bed and started fingering the cash.

"Firepower. I gotta upgrade my shit." Shane continued to stack the money. Once done, he rose to his feet. "Count that babe. Hook up five hundred G's, wrap it and put it in this bag." He tossed a dark green cloth laundry bag on the bed beside the money. "I gotta bounce for a few. Have that shit ready when I get back." Before Shaniqua could do more than nod, he was out the door.

Shane pulled out his phone and tapped the number. Cory answered on the second ring. "What up my nigga?" Shane said. When Cory responded, he immediately got down to business, telling him exactly what he needed. Once he was done, Cory assured him that he would have what Shane needed within a week. Shane hung up feeling better than he had before making the call.

With that out of the way, he drove to one of his favorite hang out joints, "Silly's Pool Hall." He had been coming to Silly's since he was a kid. The first time Ervin had brought him, Shane's eyes had grown as big as saucers. Silly's wasn't just your average place to shoot pool, although pool tables were lined up in neat rows.

Shane had been all of ten years old when he'd caught Ervin sneaking out of their bedroom window one night when he'd thought everyone was asleep. "Where are you going?" He had whispered, startling Ervin just as he'd lifted the window.

"None of yo' business. Go back to sleep." Ervin commanded, but Shane ignored him. Instead, he hopped out of bed and rushed over to the window. Goose pimples peppered his bare chest and legs from the chill of the night air flowing through the window. He stood shivering in his Superman themed under-roos. "What the hell are you doin' Shane? Go back to bed now!" Shane didn't move. He watched as Ervin's face curled up into a sneer and his fists ball up. "Don't make me punch you. Go back to bed!"

"No," Shane said. "And if you hit me, Imna go tell mama." He saw the anger flash anew in Ervin's eyes then disappear. "Let me go too." He said growing bolder with each passing second. His heart thumped hard in his little chest for fear that Ervin would ignore his threat to tell and hit him anyway.

Reluctantly, and after seeing that Shane wouldn't leave, Ervin relented. "Fine. Hurry up and get dressed and be quiet." They paddled their bikes to the downtown district with Shane trying to ask a million questions the entire time. Ervin kept telling him to shut up. When they pulled in front of the pool hall, Ervin hid their bikes in the alley then pushed his way inside. Shane was right on his heels. His eyes struggled to take in everything he saw. The sights and sounds nearly over-whelmed his young mind.

Men and women were packed inside the slightly smokey interior. The sounds of blues and jazz music filled the air. Scantily clad waitresses moved about delivering bottles of beer and glasses of alcohol to those who had ordered them. People surrounded the pool tables, poker tables and dice games that were in full swing. Several couples were dancing off near one corner.

Without pause, Ervin slipped through the throng of people and made his way towards the back room. The door was guarded by the biggest man Shane had ever seen in his young life. The dude nodded at Ervin and gave Shane a hard look, but otherwise, paid them no more attention. Ervin pushed open the door and stepped through. When Shane followed, his eyes grew even wider.

This room wasn't as large as the outer-room but was twice as packed. Ervin directed Shane to stand over in a corner and not speak or move. Shane watched as half-naked women sat at a long table piled high with a white substance that Ervin later told him was sugar and flower. The women took their time placing the stuff on scales then pouring it into small ziplock bags. The bags were then placed in stacks and given to another group of women.

Ervin moved through the women and stopped to speak to an older man sitting behind a desk. After a few moments, the man handed Ervin a brown paper bag and a wad of money. Ervin smiled then turned, and after snatching up Shane, headed back outside. That was the day Shane first learned about drugs and that his brother was dealing them.

Bringing his mind back to the present, Shane moved to one of the pool tables, snatched up a cue stick and began to play. Moments later, he was joined by the person he was there to see, Silly himself.

Silly was a tall, slender man in his mid to late fifties. He had a short cropped hair cut that hid some of the grey. He wore round, wire-framed glasses that were constantly perched on his broad nose. His skin was the color of dark storm clouds and as taunt over his bone structure as the leather pulled tightly over a drum. He wore a pair of brown slacks, brown Bailey shoes, and an open-collared white button down shirt.

"Bout time yo' young ass showed up," Silly said in his deep

baritone voice. No one knew why he had the name Silly and he never told. "You got shit taken care of?"

"Yeah, we good," Shane replied. He leaned over the table, aimed his shot and sent the cue ball snapping into the nine ball, sending it spinning into a side pocket. Straightening, he continued. "We'll have our shit by the end of the week. In the meantime, all we got to do is bide our time."

Silly nodded yet remained quiet. His mind was calculating the things he needed to get done. He looked at Shane thinking. Shane had been buying his dope from Silly ever since he and Ervin had broken out on their own and started grinding. Their business had always been straight.

When Shane had come to him and told him of Valentino's plan to take over his, network, Silly had at first, dismissed it. Yet, when he noticed all the others one by one, falling like dominoes to Valentino's schemes, he began to pay closer attention. When Shane came to him with the plan to off Valentino and the two of them take over his operation, Silly had agreed. He'd determined to be swallowed up and spit out.

"What about you? You ready on your end?" Shane asked after sinking the eight ball into the left corner pocket. He set the stick down and looked at Silly. The smile that crossed the old man's face was all the answer Shane needed.

CHAPTER THIRTEEN

Shaniqua's eyes sparkled brightly as they connected with Valentino's over the rim of the fluted glass she held close to her lips colored and glossed to shine the same deep redness of the wine she sipped. She parted them into a smile as he seductively winked at her. The two of them were enjoying a nice candlelit dinner at his penthouse apartment.

They had been having dinner a lot. In fact, this was their sixth time. After the first one, Valentino had taken her out on his yacht and made passionate love to her all night long. He vowed, in spite of his initial misgivings, about getting involved with her, to show her an entirely new side of life. The side of privilege and luxury. A side that only money could offer. The only thing he asked of her in return was that she become loyal to him, and in doing so, share with him everything that Shane did. Valentino wanted to know every move Shane made and every plan he set. Shaniqua quickly agreed.

After the dinner, they moved over to the plush sofa and

Valentino slowly laid her down and made love to her. Shaniqua felt as if she was in another world. She had never experienced a more attentive lover. Valentino took his time with everything he did, and each move, each caress, was both carefully planned and executed. Shaniqua gave herself completely over to him.

She allowed Valentino to possess her in ways that Shane nor any other lover ever had. Every touch of Valentino's lips, every touch of his fingers and every thrust of himself inside of her, solidified her loyalty. Valentino smiled to himself knowing the spell he was placing on her heart.

To prove his words to her, Valentino had set her up with a secret bank account, given her his Lakeside condo and show-ered her with jewels, expensive clothes, and shoes. He knew that she'd kept those things hidden from Shane be cause he'd advised her to do so.

Once the lovemaking session was over, the two of them lay entwined in each other's arms. Shaniqua ran her fingertips over his flawless body. "So what is our boy up too?" Valentino asked nonchalantly.

Shaniqua looked into his eyes. "I haven't been able to figure it out yet. But, I know it's something big. He took a half mil today and gave it to this dude name Cory who sells guns and shit." She stopped knowing that Valentino didn't like for his women to use profanity. "It cheapens you." He had once told her. Even still, his face seemed as if he hadn't heard her, so she continued. "He said that he needed to get himself some better equipment."

Valentino nodded slowly. He already knew who Cory was. He'd had his people check the guy out the very first time he'd heard the name mentioned. Valentino hadn't been impressed.

Cory appeared to have been nothing more than just another street punk trying to get his hustle on. But, if he had the means to move enough firepower that cost a half million dollars, then obviously his little operation wasn't so little after all. Valentino made a mental note to look more closely into the dealings Cory conducted.

More importantly though, exactly what could Shane be planning that would require him to shell out that much money? Was there some, unknown to him, war between the small-time hustlers that Shane was dealing with? Part of Valentino wanted to just come straight out and ask Shane, but he squashed it. What good would that do? Shane would simply lie about it. Plus, Valentino knew that he would be tipping his hand.

Shane would automatically know that Shaniqua was the one who had told him. No, Valentino knew that all he had to do was be patient. Shane would open up and tell her exactly what he was up too. One he did, Valentino knew that Shaniqua would come running to inform him. He leaned down and sucked on her perky nipples softly. Seconds later, Shaniqua moaned as she lost herself to him once again.

CHAPTER FOURTEEN

Tanya stood at Cory's side as they watched four of his men loading several crates into the back of the semi-truck. They were inside one of the two large hangers on the abandoned Air Force base. Cory used the hangers from time to time when he handled large shipments. He could sense Tanya's displeasure. She had been on him extra tough about stepping away from the game lately. He knew that he would eventually, but not right now. Too much paper was rolling in and way too fast, After all, he was a hustler at heart and that part of him refused to turn a blind eye to so much cash.

Tanya just couldn't shake the feeling of dread that had come over her. Although she wanted to say something, anything to get Cory's attention, she didn't want to become one of those nagging ass women men always complained about. Still, she couldn't see any rational reason for Cory to continue. They both knew that living such a life only led to jail or the grave. She had no desire to see Cory or herself, for that matter, in either place.

Plus, she wanted Cory to devote his time to fulfill his dream of owning his own business. Cory had shared with her on numerous occasions, his desire to open his own restaurant. She had encouraged him to take online business courses with her, for she had already purchased the beauty shop she'd worked at, from the owner, and renamed it, 'Tanya's Beauty Shop.' Cory had insisted on giving her the money. "After all," He had told her. "If my girl's gonna work, she may as well be working for herself."

Cory took her into his arms and kissed her deeply. "Relax babe, I promise that after this job, I'm done." He saw the relief flow across Tanya's face. His heart still leaped each time he saw her. She was so beautiful and held more class than any woman he had ever known. He knew without a doubt that she loved him fiercely too. She was his ride or die chick.

After the cargo was secure, they drove back to their place where Cory busied himself making a few phone calls. Tanya called to check on Raena but was unable to locate her. She really was worried about her girl. It had already been a week since they had visited the clinic and Raena's results still were not back. Tanya dialed up Shaniqua and the two of them made plans to get together the next day for lunch. Shaniqua assured her that Raena was okay and that she would convince Raena to join them. When Tanya hung up, she didn't feel any better, however.

She and Cory spent the night making love and talking about their future plans. Tanya had never been more content or happy in her life.

Lunch with Shaniqua and Raena was at the Lobster King Restaurant. Tanya pulled up and joined them at the reserved table. The three of them chatted about everything except what was really on all of their minds. When the lobster tails, fresh king crab and scallops arrived, they dug in with gusto, It wasn't until they were all licking the remnants of their meal from their fingers that Raena reached into her bag and pulled out a white envelope. Both Tanya and Shaniqua's eyes instantly fell on it. Raena laid it carefully on the table and all talking ceased.

Raena didn't look at them as she slowly lifted the envelope. Everything seemed to be moving in slow motion. Shaniqua reached over to touch Raena's arm reassuringly, yet Raena jerked away as if she had been shocked. "Don't..." Tanya wanted to reassure her somehow, but no words formed. She remained where she was willing her strength to her girl.

After what seemed like an eternity of silence, Raena looked at them with tears in her eyes. She gave a weak smile then in one swift motion, ripped open the envelope, snatched out the paper, then read.

HIV AB HIV % EIA
with reflectives
HIV 1/2 EIA AB SCREEN NON-REACTIVE NON-REACTIVE
A non-reactive HIV antibody result does not exclude HIV infection since the timeframe for seroconversion is variable. If acute HIV infection is suspected, antibody retesting and nucleic acid amplification (HIV DNA/RNA) testing is recommended.

Tears ran down Raena's face anew. Her hands trembled as sobs erupted from her throat. In spite of Raena's earlier reaction, Shaniqua wrapped her in her arms trying to reassure her. Tanya picked up the fallen test results and scanned them. A cry erupted from her throat as well, yet it was one of elation.

As Shaniqua clutched a sobbing Raena, Tanya read aloud the results. Pretty soon all three of them were simultaneously crying from joy and laughing. They ordered a bottle of wine and spent the next two hours toasting and celebrating life.

Afterward, they all agreed to have a girls night out and celebrate some more. They agreed to meet at a club called "Gyrations," a new spot they had wanted to check out. When they went their separate ways, they each had a new perception on life and each vowed to cherish it and live it to the fullest.

CHAPTER 15

Gyrations was an upscale club that boasted three floors. The first was dedicated to the young, urban, hip hop crowd. The music was loud and heavy with deep bass beats. Thugs and hood divas were everywhere. The guys had their tims or sneakers on, pants hanging low off their asses revealing their boxers, or skinny jeans on so tight, it was a marvel that they could move around at all. They wore wife beaters, tees or hoodie shirts and fitted ball caps on their heads. They were draped in Jewel encrusted chains, watches, rings and earrings. More than a few threw up their gang signs as they gyrated on the scantily clad women wrapped in their arms.

The women went all out in their efforts to outdo both the men and each other in the way that they danced and dressed. The place looked like a fashion show and the women were clad in more jewelry than any two or three jewelers held in their stores, All in all, the crowd was vibrant and lively.

Gyration's second floor was a techno lovers dream. The music was electrified and the light show rivaled those of even the greatest tech concert. The crowd was more "hyphy" and their attitudes reflected in the way they jumped around, danced and dressed. There was a stark contrast to the urban crowd on the first floor and far less jewelry. They were, however, far more hyped, many of them were already flying off one form of drug or another.

They were more attuned to the vibrations of the music and their bodies intertwined and pulsed with a hard edge, sexual energy that was contagious. They were pulled into the music until they became one with it.

The third floor, the one which Shaniqua and her girls chose, was far more laid back. It was a neo-jazz club with mellow bass music and a live band. Unlike the other two, no DJ was present. The crowd was mainly a more mature group with ages ranging from the mid-twenties on up. Many of the crowd were slow dancing on the dance floor or tucked away in one of the booths or at one of the intimately candlelit tables.

The sounds of a Miles Davis song being sung by a cover band, flowed through the speakers as Tanya led the way to a vacated table she'd spotted. Once seated, Shaniqua waived over a passing waitress and they gave their drink orders. By the time the drinks arrived, Raena was swaying in her seat with a wide smile on her face. Shaniqua was busy scanning the crowd, eyeing the men with an appreciative look. Tanya had her eyes closed allowing the melodic sounds to wash over her in a comforting flow.

"Girl I'm loving this spot." Raena said as the band on stage ended their selection and a tall, thin, dark-skinned sister with long locks, took her place in front of the mic. She began singing her rendition of "At last" by Ella Fitzgerald. "Imma have to come back here and get my mojo back." All three of them laughed.

"It's real nice." Tanya agreed. She was thinking of bringing Cory. She knew he would love it. She had introduced him to an entirely new level of music. She had broadened his taste in art and culture as well. They frequently visited museums, concerts, art shows, and they had even begun collecting vintage vinyl albums of all the great blues and jazz music they could find.

"Girl I don't know why y'all ass is just sitting, Imma get out on that floor and shake my thang." Shaniqua said. She bounced from her chair and approached a tall, light-skinned brother with short curly hair that she'd noticed giving her the eye from the moment they had stepped into the club. Within a matter of moments, the two of them were on the dance floor wrapped up in each other's arms.

Shaniqua whispered something in his ear and he responded by kissing her softly then pushing his tongue into her mouth. She decided then and there that the two of them would be making love before the night was over. Obviously, he had the same thought for she could feel his hard dick pressing against her body as they swayed from side to side together. She slid her hand down to it and gave ita light squeeze. When it jumped at her touch, she smiled and kissed him again.

Raena and Tanya watched their girl with mild amusement. They started talking about Raena's plans to move. Tanya offered her a job at the shop. Although Raena wasn't a hair-stylist, the girl could do a mean manicure and pedicure. Plus, Tanya wanted to add a beauty supply section that would allow her customers the opportunity to purchase all of their hair and skin care products from her at the same time. Raena would be the perfect one to manage it. Raena was excited about the prospect and readily agreed. They made plans to go over the details the next day.

Just as they began to settle back down, they both noticed an amazingly beautiful man approaching. He smiled down at them. "Hello, ladies." When they both acknowledged him, he continued. "I'm sorry for the intrusion, but I couldn't help myself." He looked at Raena. "I've been sitting over there all night captivated by you. It took all of my courage to just come over and speak. Would you like to dance?"

Raena was so taken aback by the offer, she hesitated. Mistaking her silence for uncertainty, he quickly continued. "I don't do this often. Please don't take offense, and please don't crush my ego by refusing. I don't think I would be able to handle that." He smiled and both Raena and Tanya giggled.

Instead of answering Raena placed her hand in his and allowed him to lead her to the dance floor. She glanced back at Tanya and her girl gave her the thumbs up sign. Raena smiled then turned her attention to the man holding her hand.

He introduced himself as they danced. He was thirty-three, single after having recently divorced his ex-wife and had no children. He ran his own business. He owned a used car lot where he sold pre-owned luxury vehicles. He had spent six years in the Marines fighting for his country as a combat heli-copter pilot. He'd been discharged with full honors. He'd chosen to leave the military after having been shot down while on tour in Afganistan. His ex-wife, he had discovered had been sleeping with his commanding officer.

Suddenly, he stopped himself and looked away embarrassed. He apologized as he led Raena from the dance floor, yet they did not return to the table she'd shared with her girls. Instead, they settled into one of the empty booths to continue their conversation. "I'm sorry...I was running off at the mouth. As I mentioned, I'm still sort of new to the getting-to-know-you dating scene."

Raena waved the apology away then at his urging, spoke of herself. Truthfully, she thought there was really nothing to tell. She had graduated high school, worked and struggled from day to day trying to stay afloat and ahead of her piling bills. She told him that she too had just ended a relationship with her former boyfriend, although she didn't say why. Nor did she mention her recent health scare. She ended by telling him of her new found joy and lust for life.

She also mentioned that she would begin working at her girl's beauty shop managing the beauty supply section. Nathan smiled and nodded. He had already told her his name on the dance floor. He could sense his growing connection to her and decided then and there that he really did want to know her better. Raena's thoughts mirrored his.

Tanya sat sipping her chilled glass of wine and enjoying the live band that was back on stage. They were performing a tribute to Herbie Handcock. They played a melody of his music. She scanned the crowd really enjoying the older, more sophisticated setting. Her mind, however, was still on Raena. Tanya had decided that she would do whatever she could to lift her girl's spirits and lifestyle.

As if by thought, she saw her girl sitting in the booth. Raena gave her a smile and a slight wave, then spoke to the guy she was with. He turned and lifted his drink to Tanya in response. Tanya smiled and waved at them both.

Just as she turned her attention away, she spotted a tall, handsome man entering the club. He had a dark haired, dark skinned model shaped, beautiful woman on his arm. He paused in the entrance and surveyed the crowd. Nodding to himself briefly, he escorted his obvious date, over to a reserved table and ordered the two of them drinks. The table was directly across from the one Tanya sat at.

Their seating arrangements had the man's date sitting with her back to Tanya while he sat directly across from her. Tanya was able to see his face clearly, and he hers. He glanced up and their eyes connected briefly, he gave her a smile that reflected in his eyes. Tanya smiled back. She felt an instant connection to him that had nothing to do with his good looks. When he looked Away, the feeling lingered.

Just then, the waitress was back at her table asking if she desired another drink. Tanya declined. She looked back to the table and noticed that the guy was engaged in conversation with his date. Tanya shook her head at the thoughts that swarmed in. Thoughts of her being intimate with the unknown man. She admonished herself. After all, she was with Cory and was faithful to him. She would remain so.

Suddenly, Shaniqua sat back down. The smile on her face let Tanya know that her girl was good and intoxicated. "Girl, that nigga Spinner is the shit!" Tanya looked at Shaniqua confused, then realized that she was speaking of the guy she had been dancing with. "Girl he got a can for a dick." Shaniqua laughed. "I can't wait to sample that shit."

Tanya laughed and just shook her head. She knew Shaniqua ran over men like a track star jumped over hurdles. Shaniqua always did have a way of captivating a man's attention. "Well, you better make sure you ain't biting off more than you can chew. You know Shane's ass ain't gone be happy if he finds out."

"Biting Spinner ain't on my mind even though I intend on tasting every bit of him," Shaniqua replied. "And, I ain't worried 'bout Shane. I got his ass right where I want him." She laughed out loud, picked up Tanya's wine and began to drink it.

Tanya ignored Shaniqua. Her eyes had caught that of the guy at the table once more. Again, he smiled at her. Tanya found herself caught up in the smile.

Butterflies swarmed insider her. She smiled back. Shaniqua noticed her girl's attention wasn't on her and turned to see what Tanya was looking at.

When she saw the guy, she let out a loud intake of air. The guy glanced at Shaniqua briefly, breaking eye contact with Tanya, then quickly looked away. Tanya noticed the slight look of disgust that crossed his face. Shaniqua, however, was oblivious.

"Girl that nigga is soooooo fine." She said turning back to Tanya. I saw him once before at this restaurant. He was with some other bitch then." She looked the woman over then frowning, turned back to Tanya. "The other girl was a lot better looking too," Shaniqua said out loud. It was obvious that the couple heard her.

Suddenly, the guy rose to his feet and escorted his date away from the table. He shot Shaniqua a hard look which, once again she was oblivious too, yet the smile briefly touched his lips as he looked at Tanya once more. Before Tanya could return the smile, he was gone.

Shaniqua went back to her date for the night after assuring Tanya that she would be okay. She left with him moments later. Raena joined Tanya back at the table and began talking excitedly about Dathan. The two of them had exchanged numbers and made plans to see each other again.

Raena felt her new outlook on life growing with each passing second. After about another twenty minutes, the two of them left. Raena assured Tanya that she would be at the shop bright and early. Tanya drove home in silence, yet her mind refused to allow her to stop thinking about the guy sitting at the table next to hers.

CHAPTER 16

Spinner watched with eyes filled with lust as Shaniqua stripped, then stepped over to him and wrapping her arms around his waist. She pushed her tongue into his mouth and he instinctively sucked on it. At the same time, his hands roamed over her large breast caressing them and stroking her erect nipples. Shaniqua let out a low moan then sucked on his tongue.

The two made their way over to the bed and Spinner immediately went down on her. Taking his time, he ate Shaniqua's pussy, savoring each and every inch of it. Shaniqua lay back enjoying the sensation.

Once Spinner was done, she made sure he had put a condom on before allowing him the chance to enter her. When he did, his massive penis filled every inch of her. Shaniqua let out a loud moan as he immediately started pounding inside her. There were no slow sensual strokes of lovemaking.

Just as quickly as it started, it was over. Shaniqua was more than a little disappointed. After all, not only was he rough and insensitive to her mood, and, not only was it the shortest session she'd ever had, the nigga hadn't even allowed her the chance to cum herself. He left her dry and stuck, fucked and out of luck. Plus, her pussy was throbbing as if it had a life of its own.

Spinner jumped up and immediately rushed off to the bathroom. Shaniqua slowly sat up, still in disbelief. She began to put on her clothes. "This nigga really got some damn nerves." She said to herself. She was going to make sure she gave him a piece of her mind as soon as he stepped back into the room. She was fully dressed by the time he did. Just as she opened her mouth to speak, he beat her to the punch.

"Why are you dressed? Are you leaving?" Shaniqua was so taken aback by the question, she couldn't even form a reply. "This nigga really got some nerves," she thought. She noticed that he was still naked and his body was beginning to respond to the thoughts he was having about going for round two. She decided that that wasn't going down. When he stepped closer to her, she backed away. "What's wrong?" He asked. "Why you acting like you don't want me to touch you now?"

"Cause I don't." Shaniqua blurted out. "Yo ass ain't even give me no chance to get off. And, you just gone jump up and down in my shit like that. That shit ain't even cool." She crossed her hands over her chest and took a defiant stance. "What kind of gentleman treats a woman like that?"

Spinner burst out laughing. "Girl, please. First off, I ain't never told you I was a gentleman or that I would take it easy on that pussy. Hell, it was so damn good, I couldn't help myself." He raised his hands as if to say he was sorry about it, but never said the words. "Besides, you should be proud of the fact that it was so good it made me lose all control."

"It did?" Shaniqua asked feeling proud. "You really couldn't help it?" When Spinner shook his head, she smiled to herself. "Well, I guess I do got some poppin' pussy." She moved into his arms as he reached for her again. "You really want some more?"

For an answer, Spinner took her hand and wrapped it around his erection. After stroking it briefly, she nodded. "Okay. But this time, I'm gonna be the one driving." She quickly stripped and after Spinner lay down and placed on a new condom, she straddled him slowly. Spinner fought the urge to just pound her again and allowed her to rock them both to ecstasy.

CHAPTER 17

For days Jessie couldn't get her image out of his mind. He couldn't explain the feeling that had come over him when he'd seen her sitting alone at her table three weeks ago. He had found it hard to concentrate on the things his date was saying. He had wanted nothing more than to just get up and walk over to her and introduce himself. She was by far, the most beautiful chocolate sister he had ever run across.

Although he hadn't spoken to her, he was sure that she had experienced the connection he'd felt. Just like him, her eyes seemed to have been drawn to him. It was as if two magnets had connected.

That night had been his first at Gyrations. He had purchased the club from one of his ex-business associates when the guy had run into some severe financial difficulties. Jessie had decided to view his operations first hand. He had been quite pleased with what he'd seen.

Standing, Jessie forced his thoughts of the unknown woman

from his mind and concentrated on the task at hand. He closed the laptop on his desk and rose to his feet. Lucas met him just outside his office door and fell in step in front of Jessie leading him out the front door and into the waiting limo.

Once Jessie was settled inside, Lucas took the front passenger seat and directed the driver, an older brother named Lion, to head out to the rail yard. Lion had been Jessie's driver for going on seven years. Unbeknownst to most people, he was not only Jessie's driver but was also an expert gunman.

Lion had been a firing instructor in the military, training navy seal snipers for nearly fifteen years before retiring after receiving a lucrative offer from Jessie. Whenever Jessie was conducting business, Lion always had the other party in the crosshairs of his rifle scope.

Jessie closed his eyes and thought about the report he had received from several of his informants. The fact that Valentino was making plans to push his way into Jessie's territory was no Longer in doubt. Jessie had learned that Valentino was the son of one of the most notorious mafia dons in the windy city and that they, as a family, had been branching out to other cities. Jessie knew that once they set their tentacles into something, it wasn't long before they would squeeze the life out of it. He wasn't going to let that happen to his operation.

As the limo pulled into the rail yard, Jessie could hear the sounds of the trains arriving and leaving, the noise grew tremendous as he stepped out of the car. The rail yard workers paid him absolutely no attention as he and Lucas made their way between the rusty rail cars to the small shack that served as an office. Stepping inside, he was greeted by the smell of freshly brewed coffee and nothing else. His contact was nowhere in sight.

Lucas instantly pulled his weapon and searched the place. No one was there. Jessie moved to the door, but Lucas instantly pulled him back. As he did, the door, along with the walls and every window in the place, was hit by multiple rounds from automatic weapons. The two men instantly hit the floor. Bullets bounced all around them making the air sing with their sharp whine.

The rounds ceased for a moment, then immediately picked back up. The shooters, for there were definitely more than one, raked lower and lower with their aim. The air was clogged with dust and the smell of hot lead and gunpowder. Lucas threw his body over Jessie in an attempt to shield him. Jessie pushed him off. He had also drawn his own weapon.

Once the second volley of rounds ceased, the walls looked like swiss cheese. The windows had all been blown in. Lucas sprang to his feet and rushed to one. Jessie went to the other on the opposite side of the room. Suddenly, a sharp bang sounded and one of the six men approaching the building fell as his head exploded. Seconds later, another one dropped dead with a massive hole in his chest. Jessie knew that Lion was taking them out.

Not hesitating a second longer, Jessie fired the .45 several times, drop- ping the third man and Lucas was putting rounds in the fourth. The two remaining would be assassins started firing in several directions at the same time. The building was hit again forcing both Jessie and Lucas back to the floor. One gun fell silent as Lion picked off another shooter. The final one dropped his weapon, spun on his heels and made for the shelter of the rail cars. He never made it.

Lion's round slammed into the back of his head pitching him five feet as he slammed to the ground dead.

Lucas led Jessie through what remained of the door. The rail yard was deadly silent. Not a single worker was in sight. By the time they reached the limo, Lion was in the driver's seat waiting on them. He wasted no time peeling out the moment they were in the car. Lucas was seated next to Jessie in the back.

Jessie instructed Lion to take him home. Someone had just tried to eliminate him and he needed to find out who. It had to be his contact that was supposed to have met him. But why? Jessie couldn't understand it. He was there to buy a shipment of black tar heroin from the guy that would have netted him over thirty-five million dollars. It just didn't make sense.

Once he reached home, he doubled, then tripled the guards around the house. He then locked himself into his office as he ran through his list of enemies. He made over two dozen phone calls and then flipped on the television. A news story had caught his attention. The body of his contact had been found floating the river.

CHAPTER 18

Shaniqua listened intensely as Shane outlined his plans. He, Silly and their boys would catch Valentino as he made his way to his office. They would set up a fake car accident, causing Valentino's driver to take a detour. Once he did, they would be waiting in ambush. Once Valentino was out of the way, Shane and Silly would partner up to run a new crew.

Shaniqua nodded her approval of the plan and asked if there was something she could do to help. Shane told her to contact Cory and tell him to deliver the firepower. Shaniqua was on the phone in a matter of seconds.

"Hello." Tanya's voice came over the phone. Shaniqua was slightly taken aback, but pushed on with Shane's request. He was, after all, only a few feet away listening.

"Hey, girl. What's going on?" Shaniqua said. "Is Cory around?"

"No. He just stepped out. What's this all about? What you need to talk to Cory about?" Tanya was curious as to why

Shaniqua was calling her man's phone. What business did she have with him? Hell, if the shoe was on the opposite foot, there was no doubt in Tanya's mind that Shaniqua would already be on the verge of exploding simply because some other girl had Shane's number.

"Girl calm yo' ass down. I'm just calling for Shane." Shaniqua laughed. "He wanted to make sure Cory dropped the guns and shit off."

"When?" Tanya asked a little annoyed. She wanted Cory to be completely done with the business. If Shaniqua noticed Tanya's tone, she didn't let on. Instead, she turned to Shane and asked.

"Baby when you want them dropped off?" When Shane said two days, Shaniqua relayed the information to Tanya. Tanya promised the deliver the message then hung up. Shaniqua turned back to Shane. "That's done boo. Anything else?" When he said no, she stretched out on the bed, snatched up the remote and flipped through the channels on the t.v.

Shane busied himself on the phone with Silly. It was late at night when he finally crawled into bed next to her. He wrapped his arms around her and pressed his hardness against her ass. Shaniqua didn't move. Instead, she pretended to sleep and after a few moments of trying and not being successful, Shane gave up. As he rolled over to sleep, Shaniqua allowed a sly smile to spread across her face.

CHAPTER 19

Shane stood next to Silly in the predawn gloom that coated everything in sight. It was a slightly foggy morning and the wind carried an unexpected chill. They both wore jackets for warmth over the city workers uniforms they had on. The orange and neon yellow caution vests reflected in the early morning light. The fake accident scene was already prepared and the ambush was set. Silly was on the phone with one of his guys who was the lookout for Valentino's limo. Everyone knew it would be arriving at any moment.

The scene was so meticulously planned, any and everyone would be fooled. Two cars that were twisted and mangled together, appeared as if there had been a head-on collision, were in the middle of the road. Broken glass and bits of torn metal were everywhere. Blood covered the asphalt near the heaps of metal. Flares, barriers and a detour sign had also been set up around the scene. Six men dressed as Silly and Shane stood around blowing their breath on their hands and huddled in their jackets in an attempt to keep warm.

"Let's move," Silly suddenly said. He began directing his men into position. Shane snatched up the hand-held stop sign and moved over to stand in the center of the street. Silly and three guys were moving about the wreckage as if inspecting the best way to move it.

When the headlights of the limo appeared, Shane held up the sign. The driver stopped. As the window rolled down, Shane stepped up to it. He leaned in close and began to give voice to the lie he'd prepared but was stopped as the barrel of a gun greeted him. Before he could form a thought, his head exploded as the bullet entered through his opened mouth. It exited out the back-leaving blood, gore and brain matter scattered over the pavement.

Silly turned at the sound. Seeing Shane's body sprawled and still twitching on the ground, he screamed, pulled his gun and began running towards the limo. He drew up suddenly as a hail of bullets pierced his body from all directions. They slammed into him with such force, he appeared to be performing some type of contorted tap dance. When the rounds ceased, Silly's body dropped to the ground like a wet rag.

The men with Silly were dying all around as well. After the echos of gunfire died down, the bodies of all eight men lay unmoving. Valentino stepped from the limo and looked around. All of the men Silly thought he was laying in wait for Valentino, moved into the clearing. Turning back to the lino's door Valentino extended his hand. A soft, well-manicured hand reached out and took his. He helped Shaniqua out then placed his arm around her waist.

Turning back to the approaching men, he spoke. "Clean this up. Get rid of the bodies and make sure they are never found." Turning to Shaniqua, she handed him a large briefcase. Valentino gave it to the leader of the group. "Five million dollars!" The leader smiled and nodded as he took the case. Turning to his men, he barked orders. They quickly set about removing the bodies and staged accident.

Before they could move Shane's body, however, Shaniqua moved over to it and squatted down. She looked at Shane's face, or what was left of it, for a long time. Her heart was torn. Sorrow and regret wrestled with her desires. In a moment of thought, she brushed the grief away. Besides, she reasoned, Shane could never have given her the power and luxury that Valentino offered.

Rising to her feet, she noticed the sole of one of her heels had been marred by a little of the blood on the ground. Without giving her actions a second thought. Shaniqua lifted her foot and wiped her shoe across the front of Shane's shirt. She turned and headed back to the limo.

CHAPTER 20

Shaniqua quickly settled into her new life and role as Valentino's woman.

She was always seen at his side. They were guest; at almost all the A list parties and events. The ones they were not at, wasn't due to a lack of invitation. No, it was because they spent so much time out, they decided to cut back and spend quality time alone. Shaniqua did everything in her power to become the woman of Valentino's dreams. She went all out to please him in every way. In bed, she was his every fantasy. She did things with him that she never even dreamed of doing with another man.

Valentino lavished her with expensive gifts of cars, jewels, and clothing.

Her every wish was granted. Shaniqua made him feel things that blew his mind.

She was both sassy and smart. She opened him up to a whole new world. Where he had shown her a more cultured side of life, she had exposed him to the gutter side. The downright no good, nasty ass side. Not just the hood side, but the absolute gutter. She also paved the way for him to introduce his product at a street level he had never seen before.

Shaniqua sat in the chair at Tanya s admiring the new hairstyle Tanya had just finished giving her. Raena was helping a customer, but as soon as she finished, she joined her girls. If Shaniqua was surprised at the turn her life had taken, Tanya and Raena were beyond words. They had noticed the new cars, man.

Tanya had ventured enough to ask, for everyone knew of Shane's disappearance, and Shaniqua had no qualms about letting it be known that she had moved on. Raena had been shocked beyond words. How could Shaniqua be so cold? She remembered how easily Shaniqua had moved on to Shane when Ervin had been killed.

Now that Shane was missing, Shaniqua showed not an ounce of remorse. Raena just couldn't get it. Still, although she had a lot of suspicions, she remained quiet about them.

"Damn girl, yo' ass really whipped my shit up," Shaniqua commented. She smiled her delight while patting her new, shorter, curlier hair. "Valentino's gonna go crazy." She hopped from the chair and handed Tanya four crisp hundred dollar bills. "Yo' ass is expensive girl, but shit, I ain't gone lie, you're worth every penny." She and Tanya laughed. Raena was busy lost in thought.

She was trying to figure out what had happened to Shane.

"Anyway, what's up with you and Dathan Raena?" Shaniqua asked snapping Raena from her thoughts. Raena had been dating Dathan since the night they had met at the club. The two of them were so compatible, it sometimes scared her.

"We good," Raena said guardedly. "Just taking things slow." She was just getting her life together and didn't want to push things. She had moved to a new, two bedroom condo and had purchased herself a brand new car. A Ford Mustang. She was also taking some online college courses. She wanted to become an accountant.

"Good girl. You know that man got your nose wide open." Tanya laughed. "Hell, the way you be bouncing off the walls around here, you would think he's pumping helium in you instead of dick." Both Raena and Shaniqua joined her in laughing as Tanya made exaggerated pumping noises and blew out her cheeks as if they were balloons.

"Yeah, I ain't gone lie, he got it good," Raena confessed. "Got that kind of dick yo' mama warned you to stay away from; the kind that all them old school singers like Anita Baker and Sade be singing about; the kind that be having a bitch wanting to rob banks and shit, just to please his ass."

Between peals of laughter, Shaniqua added her voice. "See, that's the kind of dick I make sho' I stay away from. The devil is a lie." All three cracked up again. "Any dick that good is way too much for me."

"Shit, they call that the love stick," Tanya said. "Have yo' ass all in love, talking about Calgon take me away."

Again, all fell out in laughter. Raena had to admit, it felt good to be so free in her spirit. She looked at her two best friends and sent up a silent prayer to God for allowing her the chance to enjoy the blessings of friendship.

After their joke fest was over, they made plans to get together over the weekend. They hadn't really had a chance to let their hair down and hang out together in some time. They all knew they needed to spend some sister time together.

CHAPTER 21

There was no mistaking the carefree sounds of laughter that carried on the wind. She looked through the trees at the picturesque scene of a father out in the park playing with his children. If it had been any other father save this one, she would have given the scene a smile. The father was without a doubt, completely enthralled with his kids. Yet, this father, with these children, gave her nothing but a sense of disdain.

"How could you fail!" She said sharply, turning in anger and addressing the tall, dark-skinned and obviously muscled man standing next to her. He held her cold gaze with a fierce one of his own. When he slowly looked away, she continued. "The plan was perfect. I can't believe you failed me. Now, what the hell am I suppose to do?" She pushed a few strands of hair that had managed to fail free of the scarf she wore, from her face. "He's too damn guarded now." Once again, her eyes turned to the scene in the park.

"Things happened." The man replied in his deep bass voice. "What can I say?" When her eyes snapped back to him, he shrugged his large shoulders then continued. "We just have to be patient. True, he's guarded now, but in time, he'll relax. He's a careful man, but even careful men slip up. When he does, we'll get him. We just have to wait our time."

"Patience!" She raised her voice slightly. "To hell with patience. I've waited long enough." She pressed down hard on the anger coursing through her body. She clenched her well-manicured hand into a fist then slowly relaxed. "I'm tired of waiting." She said in a more calmer and lower tone. "I need this done now."

The man nodded his head slightly. He too wanted to take care of the father. For, the only way he could move forward with his own plans were if the father was eliminated. Yet unlike the woman, he knew that it was far easier said than done. The man was guarded around the clock. Hell, even now, he had over thirty men surrounding him and his two children. He constantly wore a bulletproof vest and had added a man to his security detail that tasted everything that was set before him, before it ever touched his lips, including water.

He had increased the surveillance around his home, office and various businesses. He changed his schedule daily and never took the same route any- where. He didn't even share his scheduled movements with his driver. He had become almost paranoid in his actions.

Yet still, he was the most in control and rational person the large man had ever seen. He admitted to himself that he held true respect for the father and the way he conducted his business. True respect, yet still, the grudge he carried did not diminish. If truth be told, the respect he held only increased the grudge. After all, everything the father had, should have belonged to him. The money, the power, the clout, even the children, should be his. He deserved it. He'd worked harder, made moves to secure the position the father held, yet still he had nothing to show for it.

With his anger renewed, the large man swept his eyes back on the woman. He allowed them to roam over her slowly. She was still the most beautiful woman he had ever seen and the best lover he had ever known. She stood only five feet- six inches, yet she carried herself with a strength that would make the strongest of men pause. She had beautiful dark hazel, almond shaped eyes, lustrous lips, a smile that would light up the world and a mind as quick as a viper's strike.

She held a captivating power over him; One that compelled him to cater to her every whim. He knew that he was in love with her and that she, in with him. When they were together, he felt complete. He felt entirely whole. She was his breath, His every heartbeat. He longed to be with her each second of each minute of each hour of each day. Yet, she had told him, and he understood the need for both caution and patience. She had promised him that once the task at hand was done, the two of them would be together forever. He knew that they would.

"I'll take care of him." The large man said. "I promise. I'll deal with him soon." The woman stood motionless for a long moment watching the father and his children. She let the image burn itself into her memory. Finally, she turned and nodded. She touched the large man lightly on the cheek, then swiftly turned and walked away, adjusting her dark glasses on her face, as she did.

CHAPTER 22

Cory smiled up at Tanya as she wrapped her arms around his waist. They leaned onto the rail on the upper deck of the yacht and stared out into the dark waters. The sound of the party below easily carried up to them on the crisp, salty tasting breeze. He smiled to himself, feeling content with his decision. Tanya had been on him non-stop about getting out of the game and he had complied. Truth be told, he was far more ready to do so than he'd let on. The disappearance of Shane had shaken him orb than he cared to admit.

"I love you, babe," Cory said holding on to Tanya tighter. Tanya smiled up at him then gave him a kiss. Cory was glad he'd taken the steps he had. It allowed him moments like these. Moments to be with Tanya in such a beautiful setting was like a dream come true.

They, along with Raena and Nathan were enjoying a weekend cruise with Shaniqua and Valentino aboard his new yacht. When Tanya had told Cory of the plan, he was at first, reluctant. Not because he was uncomfortable or afraid of the water, although he had never set foot on a boat before, but because of Shaniqua. In truth, he never felt completely comfortable around her. That's why he rarely spent time with Tanya when her girl was around. He just didn't trust the bitch.

Cory knew that Shaniqua was a money hungry, gold digger who had once had her eyes on him. And, in truth, he admitted that there was a time when he had hungered for her. He recalled the few times he had been alone with her. That was when they were younger. Shaniqua had eagerly kissed him and allowed him to feel her up. At one point, they had nearly had sex. Only his reservations kept them from doing so. In his heart, Cory was glad that it did. Shaniqua had turned out to be, in his opinion, more than a poisonous apple killing every man tempted enough to take a bite, she had become a poisonous tree altogether.

Once Cory realized that he and Tanya were becoming serious, he had told her of his brief involvement with Shaniqua. He didn't need any skeletons from his past to pop up and ruin their budding relationship, no matter how weak the skeletons were. Tanya had assured him that she was not concerned with what he and her girl had shared in the past. She, instead, had wanted to focus her time and energy on building a solid future and foundation with him herself.

Tanya turned into Cory's arms and planted a kiss softly on his lips as she snuggled closer to his chest. Cory was about to speak but instead paused as first, Raena, then Dathan joined them on the rail.

"Nice night," Dathan said as he emulated Cory and wrapped his arms around Raena. She laughed as he whispered something in her ear.

Just as Cory was about to respond, Shaniqua and Valentino joined the group. They were followed by a waiter clad in a white jacket and bow tie, carrying a tray filled with glasses. A Moet champagne bottle was nestled in a bucket of ice as well.

"I do hope everyone is enjoying themselves," Valentino said. He smiled as they either nodded or murmured their consent. "Good. Good. Shall we toast? To new friendships and new ventures in life." He handed Shaniqua a glass as the waiter poured then took one for himself. When the others held a glass of their own, he raised his in a toast. The clinks of glasses sounded loudly as they tapped them together.

The group stood in silence for a while watching as the yacht moved effortlessly through the water, Then Valentino suddenly turned to Cory and asked for a private word. Both Cory and Tanya were startled. After a brief hesitation, Cory nodded and the two men moved to a more secluded area.

"I would like to offer you an opportunity to do business with me," Valentino said in the way of starting off the conversation. "I have quite a lucrative offer. One that would not only be profitable right now but would also allow you an opportunity to expand your business to a larger, more, shall we say, wealthier clientele."

Cory watched Valentino closely as he spoke. Although the man looked and dressed for success, and was by far, a very rich man, to Cory, he reeked of deceit. He knew that Shane had been in business with Valentino and suspected that Valentino was the one responsible for Shane's disappearance. Both Valentino and Shaniqua. Cory had no desire to become involved with the man anymore so than the casual acquaintance they already shared.

Seeing Cory's hesitation, Valentino continued. "I have to say that I am impressed with the level of professionalism of your operation. And, to be able to move such a vast amount of fire-power with such ease, only goes to show that you are a man well worth getting to know better. Why don't you take a few days to think about my offer."

"I'm no longer in the business." Cory found himself saying. "I've retired. Valentino smiled slightly which Cory ignored and continued. "I've decided that I've done that long enough. I'm now living a more leisurely life." Valentino nodded as if understanding completely, yet his next words proved that he didn't believe a word Cory said.

"Still, do give some consideration to the things I'm offering. I assure you that you will never have cause to regret our part-nership." He raised his hand slightly forestalling any more comments from Cory. "Come, let us rejoin our friends. Besides, Shaniqua can get quite upset if I leave her alone for too long." He led the way back to the group. In spite of himself, Cory found that he was very tempted by Valentino's offer. He slipped the card with the man's number on it, in his pocket and rejoined the others.

CHAPTER 23

No matter how hard he tried, Cory couldn't get Valentino's offer out of his mind. It had been over a week since they had talked and the idea consumed his thoughts. Valentino's words rang loudly like a bell. "I have a very lucrative offer. One that would not only be quite profitable right now, but would allow you to expand your business to a larger, shall we say, wealthier clientele." Cory had mentioned Valentino's offer to Tanya and of course, she had been livid. Her anger had lasted for the remainder of the cruise, and for days after. She had asked, no demanded, that Cory refuse and refuse outright. He assured her that he had.

Although his words to Valentino were true, he was done with the business, like Tanya said, they had more than enough money and it was time to start enjoying life and all it had to offer, he still thought about making more. He and Tanya had plans to travel the world. They were going to start off by going to London, then Paris and after that, Hong Kong. They were intending on going on three trips a year. Cory, in his heart, longed to do these things all the more and to do them with the love of his life.

Yet and still, Valentino's words offered him a once in a life-time opportunity. The type of money he could make would not only have him set for life, but would also guarantee that the two kids they planned to adopt, would never have to want for anything for the rest of their lives.

Pulling the card from his pocket, Cory dialed the number. When Valentino picked up and Cory identified himself, they spoke for a few moments. Cory agreed to meet Valentino to hear more of the offer. When he hung up, he was shocked to see Tanya stand right behind him. The look she held left no doubt that she had heard every word.

He went to her and attempted to take her into his arms, but Tanya instantly pulled away. "Don't Cory. Don't touch me. You lied. You promised me that you were through That you were out of the game. How could you go behind my back like this?"

"Baby...I...It's not like that. I am out. I didn't tell him that I would do anything. All I said was that I would listen to what he had to say. I just want to hear him out."

When he attempted to go to her again, Tanya pulled away once more. "Why? Why do you need to hear anything he has to say? Don't lie to me Cory, If you love me, please don't insult my intelligence. That man is a snake. He's evil. I can feel it in my soul. He's no good and dealing with him will only bring problems."

"Well if you feel that way, then why in the hell is your girl with him huh?" Cory snapped. He didn't know why he was so angry. He hadn't meant to snap at Tanya, but couldn't help it. "You ain't said shit to Shaniqua about leaving his ass alone!"

"I'm not fucking Shaniqua!" Tanya shouted, growing frustrated herself. "I'm fucking you! You are my man! You're the one I'm in love with! The one I'm planning my future with, not her! What she does is her own business. What you do is mine!" She crossed her arms over her chest.

Cory did not speak. What could he say? Tanya's words were true and he knew it. She was his woman and he knew her love was unconditional. He went to her again. This time, Tanya, in her anger, didn't pull away.

"Baby listen to me. I promise you that I'm thinking about us and the future we're planning together. I'm thinking about our kids. The ones we want to adopt. Valentino is offering me the chance to make enough money to secure their future forever."

Cory stopped Tanya before she could speak. "I know he's a no good ass man baby, and I haven't even said that I would do it. All I said was that I would hear him out. Come on love, just let me hear what he has to say. When I'm done, I'll come back and the two of us will discuss it and make a decision together." He looked at her pleadingly.

Tanya remained defiant for a moment, then after Cory smiled that smile she loved so much, she slowly relented. "You promise?" When he nodded, she finally agreed. Deep in her heart, however, she still felt as if Cory was starting a dance with the devil.

Cory kissed her long and hard then snatched up his jacket and headed for the door. "I love you, baby." He said as he reached it.

"I love you too." She replied just as the door closed on her words.

CHAPTER 24

The address Valentino gave him turned out to be that of a deli shop. Cory hopped out of his ride and made his way inside. The smell of meat roasting was strong in the air and made his stomach growl. Cory eyed the sausages, the roasted chickens, ducks and hams that hung from meat hooks behind a glass partition.

Cory noticed an elderly Italian man behind the counter and approached him. Before he could speak, however, the old man pointed to a back door with the thin cleaver he held. Cory nodded then headed for the indicated door. A slight feeling of unease washed over him but Cory brushed it to the side and wrapped his hand around the butt of his gun concealed inside his jacket pocket.

The office he entered was well lit and surprisingly, spacious. A large desk sat near one corner of the room. There were four chairs in various places. Two in front of the desk. A large oriental carpet covered the floor and faded photos lined the wall. None of this, however, caught Cory's eye. No, they had instantly settled on Valentino's smiling face. He rose from the desk and extended his hand. Cory shook it and Valentino indicated for him to take a seat in one of the two chairs while he settled back down in the leather chair behind the desk. "Cory, I am glad you came," Valentino said.

Cory nodded yet remained silent. He didn't know exactly what Valentino wanted, so he decided to allow him to bring the subject up and make his desires known. He didn't have to wait long.

"I have to say, I truly do appreciate the irony of this situation. You see, I know that you are the one who supplied the fire-power to both Shane and Silly." Valentino laughed. "Sil-ly...What an appropriate name for he truly was a silly man to have thought that he could go up against me." Cory never allowed his emotions to show on his face. His hand rested on his weapon. "Yet, I also understand that that was business." Valentino continued. "I can not fault a man for doing busi-ness, even if it was with my enemy."

"So what you want?" Cory finally said. He wanted to be done with the conversation and get the hell out of there. "I ain't come here to talk about Shane or nobody else." At the look Valentino gave him, he knew that his suspicions were right. Valentino was responsible for Shane's disappearance and most likely, that disappearance meant that Shane was dead.

"Nor do I wish to speak of the dead," Valentino stated. The look he gave Cory spoke volumes. "What I do wish is to know the source you have." Before Cory could speak, he continued. "After all, you will not be needing it anymore."

Before Cory knew what happened, he felt strong hands grab him firmly behind and wrestle him from the chair and to the ground. He lay face forward. The dusty smell of the carpet filled his nostrils. He felt a hand reach into his pocket and remove the gun.

"Now who supplies you with the weapons?" Valentino asked, lifting his pants leg and kneeling down in front of Cory. When Cory didn't answer, he stood and violently and swiftly kicked him in the face.

Pain exploded in Cory's mind as his brain registered the fact that he had been struck. He let out a wild, raw and painful cry. Blood ran from his mouth mixed with saliva. His two upper front teeth were snapped at the gum and lay on the carpet in front of him. Cory struggled against the hands that held him, yet all to no avail.

"Do you feel like talking now?" Valentino snapped. Once again, he knelt beside Cory's bleeding face. Cory strained his neck up at Valentino then spit at him. The glob of blood, saliva, and mucus landed on his eight-hundred-dollar leather shoes by Ermenegildo Zenga.

Valentino looked down at the spittle with disdain then casually pulled his handkerchief from his breast pocket and wiped his shoe. Snatching Cory by the hair, he pulled his head back then forcefully shoved the handkerchief into Cory's mouth. Valentino ignored the gags and gurgles that froth from Cory's mouth. "Get him up and take him to the back room," Valentino instructed. He turned away and headed back to his desk.

When he entered the back room, he saw that Cory was strapped down and held tightly to a large, stainless steel butcher's table in the center of the room. Cory had been stripped naked. As Valentino approached him, Cory looked up. "I'm offering you one last chance to tell me what I wish to know," Valentino said. "Give me the information and I will assure you that your death will be a swift one."

"Fuck you, bitch!" Cory spat. "Go fuck yourself." He was smacked hard across the face by one of the men who had held him down. Valentino ignored the outburst. Instead, he turned to the elderly man who Cory had seen upon entering the shop.

"Kill him nice and slow. Carve him up his pieces and feed him to the fish." Valentino stated. Without uttering another word or looking back, he walked from the room and closed the door on Cory's screams.

CHAPTER 25

Tanya cried for hours. She knew in her heart that something foul had happened to Cory. She had waited up all night for him. When he didn't return, and not once was his phone answered, she had called the police to file a missing persons report. The cops never showed to take down her words, however. She had called both Shaniqua and Raena, but both had said they hadn't seen him. When Tanya asked Shaniqua to speak with Valentino, Shaniqua reluctantly put him on the phone. Valentino admitted that he had indeed had an appointment with Cory but claimed that Cory never showed. He stated that he had waited for over an hour and a half and when Cory didn't come, assumed that Cory had changed his mind. Tanya didn't believe a single word the man spoke.

Due to the fact that she was so distraught, Tanya didn't even bother going in to work. She left Raena in charge of running the shop. She, instead, stayed cooped up in her house refusing to see or speak to anyone. She didn't answer her phone, stopped eating and slept poorly whenever she managed to sleep at all.

She spent her days crying and watching the many videos she and Cory had made or slipping through the photos she had stored on the computer. She began dressing in his clothes just to feel closer to him and get a whiff of his scent that still lingered on them. But most of all, she replayed the last conversation they had had over and over in her mind. Every word, every inflection of their tones was seared into her memory.

She had no idea how long she remained in her depressed state. Days and hours blended together in one unmemorable state of suspended time. When Tanya did finally come to her senses, she saw just how much of a state of neglect she had been in. Her entire home looked like a pig's sty. Her body was in a far worse condition. (Where once lustrous hair, hung from her head in greasy, lifeless strands. She had lost well over twenty pounds, making her look gaunt. Her clothes hung off of her and her mindset had grown to be one of utter disregard.

Tanya knew that she had to get herself back together. After all, Cory wouldn't want her to let her life, her hopes, and dreams, *QO* to waste. Somehow, thinking of him, gave her a sense of resolve and purpose. She found strength enough to began to clean up her house. She spent three days scrubbing the place from top to bottom.

Although her phone kept ringing, Tanya didn't bother answering it. She had no desire to talk. She knew that Raena was worried sick about her and vowed to call soon.

After day number three, Tanya dressed in a pair of sweats, sneakers and one of Cory's favorite fitted baseball caps, fixed herself a light breakfast, then drove to the shop. When she entered, it was a moment before anyone recognized her. Once they did, however, she was surrounded by employees and customers alike. All offered her their sympathies and asked if there was anything they could do for her. Tanya thanked them all, assuring them that she was fine, then allowed Raena to escort her the office in the back of the shop.

After assuring Tanya that everything was running smoothly, Raena turned the subject personal. "So how are you doing girl? Really. And don't yo' ass dare give me no bullshit answer."

Tanya gave Raena a weak smile then tears formed in her eyes. She didn't, however, let them fall. She stayed silent for a moment. "Bad Raena." She said. "To be completely honest, I'm doing bad. This is fucked up. Why did it have to be Cory? He was out of the game." Raena held Tanya's hand for support but otherwise allowed her girl to go on speaking. "I know Valentino had something to do with it. I don't give a damn what him and Shaniqua say!" Tanya words reflected the anger she felt in her heart.

Raena nodded. She felt the same way. She had always believed that Shaniqua had something to do with Ervin's death and that she and Valentino were behind Shane's disappearance. She found herself telling Tanya of her suspicions Tanya found herself agreeing with Raena's every word. "We got to find some way to make Shaniqua come clean with the truth," Raena said. "But how? You know her ass can be a real bitch."

"Girl, the way I'm feeling, I'm liable to beat it out of her. Tanya said truthfully. "But, you're right. I say we just confront her ass straight up." Raena had a doubtful look on her face but Tanya was adamant. "What! She ain't gone pull no gun

out and just shoot us. Plus, if she tries, I got my own gun."
Tanya reached into her purse and withdrew a .45 then quickly
replaced it. Raena's eyes bulged until they seemed as if they
would pop. "Relax girl," Tanya said. "I only carry it for protection. You know I'm not going to shoot Shaniqua. But, I am
going to get to the bottom of this though, it to Cory to do it."

Before Raena could do more than blink, Tanya had her phone
in her hand and dialing Shaniqua's number. It was answered
on the third ring. "Hello." Shaniqua sounded out of breath.
Tanya paused for a moment before identifying her- self. "Girl
it's 'bout time you called me. I have been trying to reach you
for the longest." Shaniqua said. "How you doing?"

"I'm good." Tanya lied. She was trying to figure out how to
bring up the subject now that Shaniqua was on the phone.
"Look, so what are you doing to do?"

"Well, me and Valentino were planning on just kicking it here
at home. Why? What you have in mind?" She knew that
Valentino would be slightly disappointed, but after she
explained that she was going to try and support Tanya,
Shaniqua knew he'd understand. Her heart was really torn up
about what had happened to Cory. She had Asked Valentino
about Cory's disappearance and he had sworn to her that he
had nothing to do with it. Shaniqua believed him whole-
heartedly.

"Why don't you meet me and Raena at Scores. It's time we all
had another girls nite out. We ain't hung out in a long time,
Plus, I could really use the company of my friends." Tanya
said snapping Shaniqua's mind back to the conversation.
Once Shaniqua agreed, they settled on the time. They would
get together at eight. Tanya hung up. She focused back on
Raena. The look on Raena's face was one of utter horror.
"What?" Tanya asked.

Raena was silent at first. She simply sat there shaking her head. When she finally spoke, her voice was almost a whisper. "DeJuan. He works at Scores. He's one of the DJ's there. I ran into one of his friends not too long ago and he told me." A frown crossed her face but before Tanya could make a reply, Raena suddenly jumped to her feet. "Fuck it and fuck that nigga too. He ain't gone ruin my life. Come on. Let's do something about yo' head cause that ball cap you wearing ain't doing nothing to hide that mop." She laughed and Tanya found herself laughing right along with her.

CHAPTER 26

"Scores" was a small club with a dance floor, a bar, and several chairs. The DJ's booth was tucked off into one corner and opposite that, were two doors leading to the men's and women's bathrooms. Tanya quickly found them a table near the bathrooms. She was surprised, for, in spite of its size, Scores was packed. The crowd was more of the younger, hip hop variety and not really to her taste, yet she really didn't mind.

Besides, she wasn't there to do any partying. She looked around and spotted Raena making her way over carrying two martini glasses in her hands. Raena sat one in front of Tanya. "Girl, I ain't have no idea it was gonna be this damn packed." She plopped down in a chair. Tanya simply nodded and took a sip of her drink.

She noticed Raena looking around hard at the crowd. She didn't have to be told who her girl was looking for. DeJuan was nowhere in sight. After Raena was satisfied that he wasn't, she turned back and took a sip of her own drink. "So what are you going say to her?" Raena asked.

Tanya had thought about that all day. How could she confront Shaniqua, yet not make the situation hostile? Nor, did she wish to make a scene, but she knew that she needed to get some answers. Before she could reply to Raena's question, however, Shaniqua dropped down in the chair next to her.

"Hey, girl, how you doin?" She reached over and gave Tanya a hug then did the same to Raena. "Girl, I'm so sorry about Cory." She said looking at Tanya. Tanya bit down on her anger and simply nodded her head. "Whew, I gotta get me a drink," Shaniqua said then hopped up. "I'll be right back." She disappeared into the crowd.

"Can you believe her ass?" Raena asked. Tanya just shook her head. She was struggling to control her rage. When Shaniqua had hugged her, Tanya felt as if she was being wrapped in something filthy and vile. She felt dirty all over. She found herself unconsciously brushing herself off.

Noticing that Tanya wasn't about to answer, Raena went back to scanning the crowd. Shaniqua rejoined them carrying a chilled glass of Nuvo. So what's up girl? Y'all ready to get y'alls groove on?" She gyrated her hips to the music then took a sip of her drink. "Ahhhh. That hit the spot." She continued smacking her lips. It took her a moment to notice that neither Raena nor Tanya were in the partying mood. In fact, they didn't appear to be even hearing the music, in spite of the overwhelming loudness of it. "Shit...What's wrong y'all?"

"Did Valentino kill Cory?" Tanya blurted out, unable to hold back any longer. "Did he?"

"What!" Shaniqua said startled by the abruptness of the question. "Hell no! Why you ask me some shit like that?"

"Cause we want to know!" Raena snapped. "And we want to know what happened to Shane and Ervin too. We know y'all had something to do with it so don't even try lying."

"What!" Shaniqua said again. She was so shocked by the statement, she was at a loss for words. When she was finally able to speak, she did. "Just what the hell y'all trying to say?" She looked back and forth between the two of them.

"You know exactly what the fuck we're saying," Tanya said becoming fed up with Shaniqua. "And just in case yo' ass don't, I'm saying I know you and that bitch ass nigga you fucking killed Cory!"

"Nigga fuck you!" Shaniqua said jumping to her feet. "I ain't killed nobody. Yo ass is so fucking stupid! If I did kill him, what makes you think I would just walk up in here and say it?" Tanya jumped to her feet but Shaniqua was unphased. "What? I know you ain't trying to step to me." Shaniqua said. "Nigga please_That's right, I said nigga! Bitch, cause that's exactly what yo' dumb ass is. A NIGGA! A dude with balls between yo' hairy ass legs. And for the record punk, I ain't never wanted that nigga you was getting all jealous over. What the fuck I want with a faggot huh? Cause, that's exactly what his ass was, fucking up in you. I..."

Raena suddenly snatched Shaniqua from behind by her hair and pulled Shaniqua to the floor. Both she and Tanya wasted no time in stomping and hitting her. The crowd parted and formed a circle around them yelling and cheering them on. Somehow, Shaniqua managed to land a few punches of her own. She punched Raena in the nose causing it to bleed. She managed to work her way back to her feet. The entire club had grown quiet. Even the music had stopped.

"Keep y'all damn hands off of me," Shaniqua shouted. "And bitch keep yo' AIDS infested ass away from me!" She shouted at Raena. "What! That's right bitch, I said it. A-I-D-S. You infested ass bitch." Everyone within close distance took one look at Raena with blood running down her face and immediately took a step back.

"That's right bitch." Shaniqua continued. Her eye was swelling. "You got AIDS! I switched yo' damn test results bitch. I was trying to make yo' dumb ass feel better. Well, FUCK YOU!" She turned back to Tanya and was about to snap on her but she halted. The gun in Tanya's hand made her lose all words.

The crowd finally noticed the gun and several people broke for the exit. Shaniqua however, stood her ground. "What bitch, you gone shoot me?" She laughed. Raena, recovering from the shock of Shaniqua's words, placed her hand on Tanya's arm causing her to lower the gun.

"Naw, I didn't think so." Shaniqua continued. "Fuck you Tanya and fuck you too Raena. And, fuck that nigga Cory's dead ass. Fuck Shane and bitch ass Ervin. All y'all can kiss my ass." Before either of them could reply, she turned and fled out the door.

"Come on girl," Raena said after a few moments. Tanya placed her gun back in her purse and the crowd parted as they made their way outside. Many moved because of Tanya's gun, but most did so because of the blood on Raena's face. Just as she was about to step outside, Raena turned and noticed DeJuan for the first time. She quickly averted her eyes and left.

CHAPTER 27

Shaniqua's words were like a dagger through Raena's heart. She couldn't stop crying no matter how hard she tried. She didn't want to believe a single word the bitch had said. She wanted to believe that Shaniqua had only said those things out of anger. Yet, she could no longer deny the truth of them. She held the results of her second test in her hand. Tears streamed down her face as her hands trembled.

Dathan had been trying to contact her but Raena avoided him. Once he'd stopped by her place and she had refused to allow him in. She told him that she needed time alone and to stop bothering her; to just leave her alone. Raena's heart ripped open as she watched him from her window walk away dejected. The only consolation she had was in the fact that the two of them had always used a condom whenever they made love. That, and the fact that they had never had oral sex. Dathan wasn't too big on eating pussy and that had suited her just fine for she wasn't fond of, nor had any desire to suck on any man's dick.

Dropping the test results to the floor, Raena moved into a new state of depression, yet she found that she was also mad as hell. Mad at Shaniqua, mad at the results of the test, mad at herself, but mostly, mad at the person truly responsible for placing her in this situation, DeJuan. With her anger, she found that she had an intense desire for revenge.

Raena quit her job at the shop, telling Tanya that she had no longer had the heart to deal with it. Tanya had understood and vowed to be at Raena's side no matter what. And, although she had wanted to spend some time with her, Raena wouldn't allow it. She explained to Tanya that she just needed her own space for a while; needed time to come to grips with it all. After all, her seemingly second chance at life had been brutally snatched away from her.

Sitting down at the table, Raena began to plot. She wrote down everything she thought she would need. Once done, she gathered her purse and headed out the door. She returned almost four hours later with her arms loaded with bags and wasted no time in getting to work.

Once finished, Raena hardly recognized the person staring back at her in the mirror. She wore a long, dark, auburn wig that reached the center of her back. The contacts she'd placed in her eyes had changed the color of them from dark brown to a light hazel. The extra padding in her bra turned her from a 36-C to a double D. Raena had also put on black, tight, ass-hugging, leather pants with thigh-high stiletto boots, a tight brown blouse and wore a look that would invite any man with enough courage to come and have his way with her.

Snatching her purse, Raena looked at her watch and made for the door. It wasn't long before she was seated at a table near the DJ's booth back at Scores. That was where she remained the entire night. She did take the opportunity to dance with a few guys but whenever one tried to take an interest in her, she quickly dissuaded them. No, her eyes were on one man and one man alone, DeJuan.

She made it her business to flirt with him, catching his eyes with hers and both winking her eyes and licking her lips at him seductively whenever their eyes connected. At one point, she had even gotten up and handed him a napkin she had written a note on asking for him to meet her out in the parking lot once the club closed. After that, she sipped her ginger ale and waited for the time to pass.

When DeJuan's voice came through the speakers letting everyone know that he was playing the final song of the night, Raena stood, gave him a smile and pointed towards the door. DeJuan nodded his understanding and moved to start packing up his equipment.

Raena didn't have long to wait. Ten minutes after she'd stepped outside, she spotted DeJuan making his way over to her. He looked appreciatively at the new BMW she leaned against. "So what's up baby?" He asked moving to stand directly in front of her. "You called and here I am."

Raena looked him up and down seductively. Taking her hand, she lightly rubbed it over his skinny chest. Inwardly, she was shocked. DeJuan had always had a fantastic physique. That had been one of the reasons she had been so attracted to him. Now, from the feel of his chest, he was nothing but skin and bones.

Still, Raena didn't allow that to give her pause. She was on a mission and was determined to see it through. "If you ain't too busy, why don't we go back to my place." She said in an exaggerated accent. "I want to see if you can spin me as well as you do your records." Without waiting for him to reply, she opened the driver's door and sat behind the wheel.

DeJuan didn't need any more urging. He quickly moved around the car and slid in the passenger's seat. He couldn't believe his luck. This girl was not only fine as hell, but she was obviously rolling in a nice stack of money. De- Juan knew that if he played his cards right, all she had would eventually be his. After all, she was all over him, and they had just met.

The entire ride to her place, Raena did little talking. She was content with letting him run his mouth. That was one thing that definitely hadn't changed about his ass. When he did manage to ask a question, Raena would simply mumble an answer and DeJuan would continue on. She listened hard for the one thing he never mentioned. He never told her that he had AIDS. Nor, did he ask her. Instead, he lied continuously about all the things he would do to her in bed to fulfill her every fantasy. Raena just smiled seductively and nodded.

As they pulled up to her condo, DeJuan let out a low, appreciative whistle. Raena just smiled. She had told him that her name was Sylvia. DeJuan had laughed and continued to tell her all about himself.

As they entered the house, Raena told him to make himself comfortable. DeJuan wasted no time in doing just that. As she disappeared into the bedroom, he moved over to the bar and poured himself a drink, then walked around slowly checking the place out. He loved everything he saw. Yeah, he said to himself, she definitely had money.

His inspection was interrupted however when she called him into the bedroom. The sight that greeted him stole his breath away. Raena stood nearly naked in a fishnet dominatrix outfit. A soft leather whip was in her hands. She knew that this outfit was exactly what was needed to turn his ass on completely. He had tried on several occasions in the past, when the two of them were together, to get her to get kinky with him. Each time, Raena had adamantly refused. Bondage was not her thing.

She smiled to herself as DeJuan instantly became hard. She noticed the imprint of his stiff dick in his jeans. "Damn baby." He said breathing hard and stepping into the room. He began to undress without her urging. "Take me ma. I'm all yours." He laughed and lay down on the bed.

"Don't speak!" Raena snapped and tapped him lightly across the chest with the whip. DeJuan let out a low moan. "Don't move!" She reached down and pulled open a bottle of body wax and set it on the dresser. The entire time she made sure he maintained a full view of her ass and pussy mound between her legs. She also set a bottle of chocolate sauce next to the wax. "Move to the head of the bed." Once again, she hit him with the whip. This time, however, the lash had a little sting. DeJuan leaped to comply.

As he did, he watched her place a small wooden box on the foot of the bed. She then crawled up his body. Her pussy rested just above his belly button and her breast swayed back and forth in his face as she leaned down. Raena allowed him the pleasure of taking one into his mouth as she reached into the drawer on the nightstand and removed a pair of hand-cuffs that were covered in a red fuzzy material.

DeJuan never saw the first one as she snapped it around his wrist, then to the headboard. When he managed to look up, she snapped the second one swiftly around his other wrist, and just as quickly to the headboard. His arms were stretched wide.

A brief look of panic filled DeJuan's eyes but he immediately replaced it with desire as Raena stroked his throbbing manhood. She allowed him to continue to suck on her nipples for a brief moment before she pulled her breast free of his mouth and slowly ran the whip across his body as she crawled down it.

Switching positions, she placed her pussy in his face. DeJuan moaned as she stroked him. He wasted no time in dipping his tongue into her hot moistness. He wasn't aware of the leather ankle restraints that had been placed on his ankles until she suddenly stood up. He tried to move but it did no good. DeJuan lay spread eagle on the bed.

"Baby..." He began but cut his words as she took some of the body wax into her hands and moving up his body, began to rub it on his chest. DeJuan moaned out loud. "Ohhh baby, that feels so good." Raena didn't comment as she continued to rub wax all over his body. DeJuan was so stimulated by the massage, his dick felt as if it was about to explode.

"Does that feel good to you baby?" Raena asked DeJuan. He nodded with his eyes closed. Suddenly, they snapped open.

"Raena?" He asked in shock. He noticed that she had stopped speaking with an accent. "Raena is that you?" He shifted but the binds held him tight. Raena laughed at his struggles then she began to remove the disguise she'd worn.

"Oh, that's right." She said. "I forgot to tell you." She taunted him. "I'm not really who yo' ass thought I was, but don't you worry, we're still gonna have some fun."

DeJuan's eyes grew even wider as she peeled the contacts from her eyes. "Shit, I won't be needing these." She tossed them to the floor. "After all, I can see just fine."

"Raena? Raena baby, what are you doing?"

Raena ignored the question for a brief moment as she opened the wooden box and removed several items. The first was a long whip with six separate leather tips. DeJuan let out a low moan when she held it up for him to see. The second item was a small wooden mallet used to tenderize meat, and the third was a tiny, thin wire with three loops on it. She placed them on the bed.

Before DeJuan could do any more than blink, Raena turned up the volume on the radio. Up until she did, he hadn't even noticed that it was on. "Raena... Baby, talk to me. Girl, what are you doing?"

Instead of answering him, Raena picked up the wire and moved over to his penis and swiftly placed one loop over each of his nuts and the third over the head of his penis before moving it down to the base. She held the end of the wire in the palm of her hand. She gave it a slight tug causing the loops to tighten around his now limp dick and balls.

Panic filled DeJuan's eyes as Raena stepped to the head of the bed still holding the wire. She picked up a gag she'd hidden and commanded for him to open his mouth. When DeJuan refused, she gave a harsh tug on the wire. The pain that shot up through his nutts and penis caused him to scream out. That scream, however, was snuffed out as Raena shoved the gag into place roughly, then secured it with a tie string around his head.

Raena spoke. "So how does it feel nigga?" She gave the wire another tug sending pain throughout his body. "Yeah, take it! It feels 'bout as good as these damn AIDS you done gave me bitch!" Raena tugged once again violently. She ignored his muffled screams.

She took pleasure in the beads of sweat that formed on his forehead. Releasing the wire, she picked up the whip and after going through a few test swings, brought it down viciously across DeJuan's naked body. DeJuan screamed so loudly and with so much force, he nearly passed out. Raena simply smiled. The wax kept the skin on his flesh from tearing thereby allowing the beating she was going to give him to last that much longer.

Raena took her time working the whip up and down his body. He bucked and screamed yet all to no avail. The sounds that the gag didn't conceal were muffled out by the music from the radio. When she was finally finished beating him, she had worn her arm out and was panting from the exerted effort. Large red welts had risen all over DeJuan's body covering him completely. "That's for all the women you've lied too; For all the lives you've ruined with that lying ass tongue of yours." She snapped.

Taking her time, Raena moved over to the nightstand and picked up the chocolate syrup bottle and pulled open the cap. She smiled evilly at DeJuan as he looked back and forth between her and the bottle. "Oh no baby, you gets no chocolate delights." She laughed at his confused look then in one swift motion, poured the contents all over his body. DeJuan screamed himself horse as the industrial grade alcohol burned its way into his welts. Raena laughed at his pleading look.

After all the bucking had stopped and his whimpers had ceased, Raena moved back to the end of the bed and took up the wooden mallet in her hand, and the wooden box in the other. She positioned herself between DeJuan's legs. Sitting back on her heels, she took her time lifting his limp penis and nutts and after positioning the wooden box just to her liking, carefully placed them on top of it.

"Now for the best part baby, I'm gonna help you bust a nutt." She smiled again to herself. DeJuan realizing what she was doing, started to struggle with all the energy he had left in his feeble body. Just as he did, however, Raena lifted the mallet and viciously and violently brought it down with all of her might, smashing his left scrotum.

The deadly scream DeJuan unleashed could not be contained by the gag. Tears streamed down his face and his body jerked so violently, the entire bed rattled.

"What you say, daddy?" Raena mocked. "Oh, you're ready for round two huh?" DeJuan shook his head back and forth pleadingly. "Okay, boo...I'm gone let you get a double up." She slammed the mallet down on his right testicle. Both blood and spittle oozed from the gag shoved into his mouth. DeJuan's body never knew such intense pain.

He bucked and jerked so intensely, his muscles cramped. He prayed to God to spare him from any more pain, and to please just let him die. His prayers, however, did not reach heaven.

Raena lost herself and began beating the mallet up and down his limp penis. Each wave of pain grew more and more agonizing. DeJuan hoped he would pass out but the rapid pounding of the mallet kept him from doing so. By the time Raena stopped, his entire private area was nothing but a bloody lump of ripped and torn flesh.

Raena moved off the bed then took out her new gun. It was a .44 magnum. She meticulously placed two bullets into the chamber. "Now it's time for me to put you to bed boo. Say goodnight."

Before DeJuan could do more than blink, Raena blew a hole in his head. Blood, bone and brain matter splattered the wall. She knew that although the music had hidden his cries, it would do little to hide the sound of the gun going off. Without wasting another thought, she placed the barrel into her mouth, closed her eyes and pulled the trigger for the second time. Death enveloped her.

CHAPTER 28

Jessie's mind knew no rest. Try as he might, he could not find out who had tried to have him killed. As a result, he became even more cautious in his movements. His only source of consolation came with being in the presence of his kids. He had Lucas go and gather them up. He never entered Olivia's home, nor did he have a desire to do so. He never wanted to lay eyes on the bitch again.

Sitting in the back of his new bulletproof limo, he scanned the contents on his iPad. Soon, he became lost in the story he was reading of some woman who had tortured then mutilated her lover before killing herself. The gruesome photos that accompanied the story, was enough to turn his stomach.

Jessie shut the iPad off and laid to the side. Glancing at his watch, he noticed that he had been waiting well over ten minutes. Sighing his frustrations, he knew that this was probably one of Olivia's ways of trying to get under his skin. She took every opportunity she could to spite him and making him wait was just another one.

Finally, after Jessie seemed as if he had reached the limits of his patience, the front door opened and Lucas emerged with Jackson and Aniah in tow. Jackson was his usual vibrant, energetic and talkative self, but Aniah was unusually quiet. She walked to the car with her head down. Jessie assumed that her mother had once again been scolding her.

Jessie just couldn't understand Olivia and how she didn't seem to notice that Aniah was such a sensitive girl. He vowed to pay Aniah a little more attention in hopes of lifting her spirits.

Jackson jumped into the seat and in an excited ball of questions began to speak. "Hey dad, are we going to the space museum today? Can we ride on the subway? Dad, mom says zebras are horses. Are they?" At seven years old, he was every bit as adventurous and curious as Jessie knew he must have been. Jessie smiled down at his son marveling at just how much Jackson looked like him.

While Jackson continued his stream of questions, Aniah climbed into the car and huddled in the far side of the back seat. After briefly looking at her dad, she mumbled a soft and weak "Hi daddy." Jessie's attention immediately turned to his daughter. Aniah avoided eye contact and instead, bruised herself playing silently with her doll.

"Aniah...Come over here." Jessie said softly, pulling her close to him. When she was in his arms, he continued. "What's wrong baby girl? Talk to your dad." He gently lifted her face towards him with his finger under her chin. Aniah began to cry. Jessie felt his heart tear as she averted her eyes. Before either Jessie or Aniah could say anything, Jackson spoke up.

"She's mad cause mamma yelled at her." He smirked, finding

his sister's misery quite amusing. Jessie shot his son a hard look that caused his laughter to cease. Jackson looked out the window as the limo sped down the street. Noticing that the private partition wasn't in place, Jessie hit the button and silently watched as the tinted window slid into place. He wanted to know the extent of what was going on with his daughter and he wanted his words to remain strictly between him and his children. Lucas and Lyon did not need to hear what he had to say.

Turning back to Aniah, he tried to comfort her. "Baby, tell daddy what's wrong. Did mommy yell at you?" Aniah remained silent, yet the look in her eyes told him that Jackson had told the truth. "Aniah, why did mommy yell at you? Did you do something bad?"

Still, Aniah remained quiet. Jessie was at a loss. This was so unlike his daughter. He scooped her up and sat her in his lap. Jackson was busy with playing with the remote to the television. Jessie left him to it.

Aniah remained closed lip in spite of all his efforts to get her to talk. Eventually, he gave up, resolving to simply show her the best time he could in the hopes that eventually she would cheer up.

Jessie had Lion take them first to the space museum as he had promised Jackson. With his bodyguards spread out around them, they walked around looking at the exhibits. Jackson was so thrilled, he could hardly contain himself. He ran from display to, display awed at the planes, fighter jets and space shuttles.

Jessie busied himself with taking pictures, yet he still noticed Aniah's sullen mood. He picked her up and carried her in his arms. He was slightly surprised at the level of intensity in which she held on to him. Hating to have to do so, Jessie made a mental note to speak to Olivia when he returned the kids.

After the museum, they ate slices of pizza in the park and afterward, visited the toy store. All three cars, the one they rode in, as well as the two SUV's that the bodyguards were in, were filled with packages. Jessie had allowed his children to go wild in the store. Aniah, however, showed little interest. She only seemed to have brightened somewhat when she took her time choosing a new doll.

The last stop on the day's agenda was the zoo. Both Jackson and Aniah had begged to be able to see the animals at night. Plus, the zoo would be having a bird show in the new sanctuary that had been built. Both children were excited to see the eagles. Along with the show, they would get the chance to eat dinner outside.

As they took their seats in the stands, Aniah crawled into Jessie's lap and the lights dimmed. She clutched her new doll in one hand and her other doll in the other. Jessie noticed the intensity of the look she was giving him. The sorrow in her eyes crushed his soul. He had tried on several occasions to get her to open up to him about what was going on but Aniah was stubborn if nothing else.

In spite of himself, Jessie was captivated by the flying skeptical that the birds made. He, along with with everyone else, ooohed and ahhhed at the acrobatic tricks, the light show and the singing parrot. After the show was over, and when the house lights clicked back on, Jackson was wide-eyed and so full of excitement, Lucas, who was seated next to him, was having a hard time keeping him calm.

Jackson wanted to run after the trainers while at the same time, asking if he could have a bird of his own. When Jessie looked at Aniah, she was smiling for the first time. Jessie sighed in relief. They left the arena and moved through the ape town section to watch the gorillas and chimpanzees. Jackson held Lucas hand tightly and the two of them were slightly ahead of Jessie and Aniah.

Suddenly, Jackson cried out. Both Jessie and Aniah jumped. Jessie assuming the worse, snatched Aniah up into his arms while looking around for the danger. It took him a moment to realize that Jackson's scream was accompanied by his laughter. Jackson was pointing in the direction of the large enclosure that housed several silverback gorillas. Lucas was at Jackson's side laughing as well.

Looking over, Jessie noticed a large male gorilla mounted on top of a smaller female penetrating her with his penis. The male was moving fast on top of her while the female was submissively allowing it.

Jessie quickly looked away and attempted to shield Aniah's eyes as well. She was wide-eyed. Fear was plastered on her face. Jessie thought the entire scene would be comical except for the fact that he noticed his daughter was truly on the verge of becoming hysterical.

Taking her, he quickly walked away in the opposite direction. Lucas gave him a quizzical look but Jessie shook his head. He needed to be alone with his daughter. Every instinct within him was screaming a warning, telling him that something was wrong. He intended on finding out exactly what it was.

Sitting on a bench, Jessie hugged Aniah to him for a few moments then spoke softly. "Aniah. It's alright. Daddy is right here. The monkey wasn't hurting the other one. Don't cry. It's alright, I promise you." He smiled in an effort to reassure her, yet it only caused her to cry even more. Jessie looked around for something, anything to say but his mind came back with nothing.

"Baby what's wrong? You can tell me. You know that you can tell me anything right?" Aniah shook her head yet remained silent. "Come on. Tell me why you've been so sad all day."

"I can't," Aniah said in a soft whisper. She looked up at Jessie but otherwise remained silent. Her small lips quivered with the effort to keep from crying again. "I can't daddy. I don't want to get in trouble no more. Mommy said I have to learn to keep my mouth shut."

Jessie was both shocked and appalled by Aniah's words. What was Olivia up to? Why would she talk to a six-year-old girl, her own daughter for that matter, like that? Jessie sat Aniah straighter on his lap and looked her in the eyes. "Baby, you know daddy Loves you right?" He waited until she nodded, then continued. "And daddy promise you right now that I won't let nobody hurt you. Not even mommy. And, you know daddy always keeps his promises right?" Again, Aniah nodded. "So daddy promise you that if you tell me, I will keep you safe."

"But who's going to keep you safe?" Aniah asked. Jessie smiled at her concern for him, yet she didn't return the smile. "Seriously daddy, mommy says that if I ever tell you what her and uncle Lucas be doing, she would hurt me and then you would get hurt too. I don't want you to get hurt."

"Daddy won't get hurt baby. I promise you. Now, what did mommy and uncle Lucas do?" He already had a picture forming in his mind from Aniah's words and her reaction at seeing the gorillas going at it. Yet still, he needed to hear what his daughter had to say. He didn't have to wait long to find out.

"They were doing like the monkeys. I...I didn't mean to daddy." Aniah paused yet when Jessie urged her, she continued. "They were in mommy's room naked and he...Uncle Lucas was on top of her. I thought he was hurting mommy so I screamed real loud and ran in the room telling him to stop. When Uncle Lucas jumped off of mommy, she yelled at me and...Uncle Lucas grabbed me by my arm. He...He hurt me when he pulled me over to mommy. Mommy spanked me and told me to shut the hell up. She said that I better not cry."

Aniah paused as tears welled up in her eyes. Jessie wanted to comfort her so he gave her a tight squeeze yet allowed her to continue. "Mommy said to keep my mouth shut and not to say anything to you. She said that if I did, I would get hurt and uncle Lucas would hurt you." Aniah stopped all of a sudden and looked around frightened. Jessie was in such a rage, he could barely contain it.

Taking Aniah by the hand, he assured her again that everything would be okay. He also assured her that she had done the right thing by letting him know. He asked her not to say anything else about it and made her promise that she wouldn't let her mother know that she had told him. Aniah was more than happy to keep quiet.

Rising to his feet, he led Aniah back over to the others. He intentionally avoided Lucas inquisitive looks and headed for the exit. He carried Aniah in his arms and held Jackson by the hand. Jackson was asking if they could come back again. Jessie nodded yet otherwise remained silent.

Once they reached the cars, he handed Aniah to one of the bodyguards and watched as Jackson climbed in after her.

Jessie turned to Lion, gave him a slight nod of his head and headed off a short distance. After speaking briefly, they returned to the cars.

Lucas walked up to meet them. Without pause, Jessie reached back and slammed his fist into Lucas's face. The big man clutched his jaw in rage. When he looked back at Jessie, his eyes fell on the barrel of the gun Lion had pointed at him.

CHAPTER 29

Olivia was more than a little surprised to find Lion at the door returning Jackson and Aniah. She was sure that it would have been Lucas. After all, he was the one who always brought them home. "Uh...Where...Where is Lucas?" She asked while shooing the kids further into the house. "Why didn't he bring the children?"

"The boss needed him to run an errand." Lion lied. "But...He asked me to tell you that he would be by soon to see them later." Lion pointed at both Aniah and Jackson. Before Olivia could say any more, Lion turned and walked away.

"What did she have to say?" Jessie asked as Lion moved to the driver's door. Jessie was leaning on the side of the car watched in with an impassive eye as his guys surrounded the area. He was beyond livid. He wanted nothing more than to just walk up and put a bullet in Olivia's brain. Yet, he knew that would not be his wisest move.

"Asked about Lucas." Lion said with disdain. "I told her what you wanted me to say and walked away. She was shocked to see me instead of his ass." Jessie nodded then hopped into the back seat. As Lion pulled away from the house, he saw Olivia looking out the window. Jessie smiled to himself and leaned back.

The ride was a short one. As Lion brought the limo to a stop in front of one of Jessie's businesses, Established Meats, which was a large industrial size stockyard, which lay just a few miles from the inner working so the city, Jessie stepped out.

The stockyard once belonged to a conglomerate group of cattle ranchers from Texas. They had raised prime beef cows for human consumption. When two of the owners, both who combined, made up the majority ownership of the business, had become indebted to Jessie to the tune of over forty-five million dollars each. They had gladly turned over their shares of the business, along with the cattle they raised, and ten million dollars they held jointly in the bank, in exchange for their lives and the lives of their families.

Jessie, for his part, never had any intentions of harming their families, yet he did not let that be known. After all, he did have a reputation of being quite brutal to those who opposed him.

Stepping from the limo, Jessie carefully made his way to one of the large holding pens. The stockyard was deserted for the time being. It always was at this time of the year. This was one of the two times the county inspectors came to check for code violations and to see if all the state regulations were being adhered to. The other inspection happened at the height of the selling season. The yard would be closed for the entire week.

Lucas was held bound by large leather straps. He was stripped naked and suspended between two posts with his arms and legs stretched wide. His face was bloodied from the few blows he'd received as he tried to resist, yet was other-wise unharmed. He glared at Jessie with hate-filled eyes as he approached. Lion was only a step behind his boss, yet Lucas didn't bother with shifting his eyes towards him.

Jessie held a long-handled cattle prod in one hand and a leather whip in the other. The whip was tipped with small metal barbs. Lucas laughed as he noticed it, then sneered at Jessie once more. Jessie ignored both the sneer and the laugh.

Once, in rage, he flicked his wrist and sent the tip of the whip lashing out across Lucas taunt, muscled chest. The metal barb bit into his flesh as if it was made from butter. The scream that issued forth from Lucas' throat was loud enough to wake the dead. All thoughts of laughter or sneers fled from his mind.

"Your bitch ass already know how this is going to go right?" Jessie asked sarcastically. "Now, I'm going to show you right now exactly how much I will be enjoying this." He lashed out with the whip a second time, then jerked his hand back. The metal barb snatched a chunk of flesh from Lucas' shoulder. Lucas howled like a bitch in heat. "Naw nigga. I don't want to hear you cry- ing now. You wasn't crying when you ran behind my back. When you were fucking that no good bitch." Jessie ignored the sounds of astonishment from the men surrounding the place who were within earshot. Up until now, none of them, save Lion, had known what Lucas had done to turn Jessie on him. Many had assumed that it was probably because Lucas had gotten caught stealing or something.

"No. Not right now." Jessie continued. "We'll have plenty of time for you to talk. Right now, however, it's time for you to suffer." Jessie lashed out with the whip once more, this time taking a chunk of meat from his right thigh. The screams that echoed throughout the place was filled with agony. Jessie nodded to himself. He knew that Lucas would regain his sense of resolve and become stubborn, refusing to give him the satisfaction of hearing him cry out again. That was exactly what Jessie wanted, for he knew that the longer Lucas held out, the longer the torture would last.

Taking the cattle prod, Jessie began to touch Lucas chest and stomach. Lucas bucked with the force of the electric jolts that coursed through his body. At one point, he both vomited and urinated on himself. Jessie ignored this as well and continued to meticulously prod Lucas with the rod. When Lucas nearly fainted from the pain, Jessie paused. "Now your bitch ass can start to sing. So, why don't you start by telling me why you went behind my back like that?"

All thoughts of resisting had been freed from Lucas' brain by the stings of the prod. However, his anger and hatred for Jessie remained, he wanted nothing more than to hurt Jessie just as badly as the prod and whip had hurt him. Yet, he knew that the only way to do so was through his words. He laughed, causing both blood and vomit to spew from his mouth. Yet, before Jessie raised the prod again, Lucas spoke.

"You're a dumb ass nigga Jess." He taunted, knowing just how much it grated on Jessie's nerves to be called that. "A real dumb motherfucker. You think I give a shit about you or them nasty ass brats of yours? Hell naw! Nigga, fuck you and them."

Jessie had the urge to lash out at Lucas for disrespecting him and his children, yet he restrained himself. He knew that Lucas was trying to goad him. Jessie wouldn't give him the satisfaction. In fact, he knew that by doing the opposite of what Lucas wanted, he would be forced to talk more, and in doing so, reveal more and more. That was exactly what Jessie wanted.

When Jessie stood unphased, Lucas spat on the ground then continued. "Yeah nigga, I know yo' ass is mad, no matter how much you try and act like you're not. That's just like the bitch ass nigga you are!" He heaved another glob of spit at Jessie, yet it fell far short of its target. "Fuck you nigga. Yo' ass ain't shit! And, you ain't never gone be shit."

The effort of unleashing his anger at Jessie caused Lucas to heave a deep breath before he could continue. Jessie stood impassively. "You're just like your punk ass daddy, walking around like y'all better than everybody else. My pops was right. Both of y'all ain't nothing but a bunch of bitches."

Involuntarily, Jessie clenched his jaw in anger and Lucas noticing, laughed. "What, you mad cause a real nigga like me is telling the truth? He was a bitch and yo' ass is too. Like father like son! And speaking of sons, that little bitch ass one you got ain't even yours." Lucas laughed again seeing the pain his words caused in Jessie's eyes. "Yeah, that's right. You see, Marcus wasn't the only one fucking that funky cock bitch! I've been dipping in that shit from day one you stupid ass motherfucker. Me and every other nigga in town."

Jessie felt his anger rising higher with each passing moment, yet he knew that the words Lucas was speaking weren't true. Well, at least those pertaining to his children, for he had immediately gone and had DNA tests done on both of them the moment he had discovered Olivia's cheating. His mind had been assured long ago about them being his.

In truth, what had angered him was the fact that Olivia had

flaunted herself; giving herself to every man with a hard dick. For not the first time, Jessie regretted not heeding his father's words when he had advised him not to fall in love with Olivia.

Jessie focused his mind back on Lucas, however, for he was still speaking. "Yeah, that's right. Even my old man might be the father of them little shits. He was tapping that ass too." Lucas laughed and spat again enjoying the torture he thought his words were giving Jessie. Jessie found himself bursting at the seems with rage. He lashed out with the whip catching Lucas across the right eye. Pain exploded anew in Lucas' brain and his body rocked with the force of the blow.

"Nigga watch your mouth. Your sorry ass pop wasn't shit. He wasn't nothing but a no good, two-timing punk ass nigga, just like you. That's why my dad offed his bitch ass." Jessie saw the shock his words caused Lucas, in his eyes. Lucas snapped his head up. This time, it was Jessie doing the laughing. "That's right nigga. Oh, don't tell me you really believed that shit about Felix being shot and killed in a drive-by." Jessie relished in the pain on Lucas' face. "Nigga, please. You really are a stupid ass nigga."

Jessie took a step closer to Lucas so that he was right in his face. "Naw nigga. I killed his bitch ass. Put a bullet right between his eyes." Jessie took the end of the whip and poked it between Lucas' eyes. Eyes that were filled with rage. "See, just like you, yo pops wasn't shit. I caught his ass trying to steal from us. He thought he was so slick. His ass learned better though. I begged pops to let me knock your noodles too, but he wouldn't. Hp felt as if he owed you something, some type of mercy. After all, it was Felix who tried to fuck over us." Jessie stepped back seeing rage moving through Lucas so hard, his suspended body trembled all over. "Well,

I'll agree with you on one thing, pops was wrong. Wasn't shit about you loyal."

Before Jessie could say anything more, Lucas screamed, yet it was not a pain induced one, or at least not the pain caused by the whip or cattle prod. No, it was caused by the revelation of Jessie's words.

Lucas spewed forth a stream of curses. "Bitch nigga! I should have offed yo' ass a long time ago. I should have listened to Olivia when she told me to let yo' stupid ass bite the bullet." He spat at Jessie, never caring what his words revealed. "That's right bitch. I should have let yo' ho cake ass eat it in the rail yard that day."

In fact, he had planned too. Olivia had finally convinced him to help her get rid of Jessie, claiming that with him out of the way, and with his kids, the two of them would and could easily take over and run the operation. Lucas, both jealous and envious of Jessie, had finally agreed. He had set the entire thing up. He'd hired the hit men, picked the location for the meeting and had even killed the contact that was supposed to have met them. It was only after the bullets started ringing out that he had, on impulse, given in to a moment of regret and pulled Jessie to safety. He hated himself for falling weak at that moment.

Jessie stared at Lucas in disbelief. Not once, had he even considered that Lucas could be behind the hit. Why would he? After all, Lucas was around him nearly twenty-four hours a day and had ample opportunities to try and kill him. No, he had been absolutely sure that it had been one of his enemies who had ordered the hit. Jessie's anger finally exploded.

Before he knew what he was doing, his hands had the whip whisking back and forth through the air so quickly, it was barely visible. The barb was ripping the flesh from Lucas and sending it flying through the air in bloody chunks. Lucas's screams were muffled by the rage flowing through Jessie's body. When he'd finally exhausted himself, Lucas looked like nothing more than another bloody slab of meat hanging from one of the hooks at Jessie's meatpacking plant.

With his anger spent, Jessie took one final look at the shredded mass of flesh that had once been his right-hand man, then turned away. Handing both the whip and cattle prod to Lion, who had remained standing at Jessie's side unshaken and unmoved the entire time, he spoke. "Finish this piece of shit!"

Lion nodded once, dropped the whip to the ground and taking the cattle prod, shoved the prong side first, up Lucas's ass. Amazingly, Lucas managed to scream. They shook the entire pen areas as the electricity bit at him from the inside. Jessie ignored them as he stepped from the pen and headed back to the limo. He had one more score to settle and this one was more personal than any other.

CHAPTER 30

Olivia was surprised at the sense of relief she felt upon receiving the text message from Lucas. It had been almost a week since the shock of having Lion at the door instead of him. At first, she had been livid. How dare he not show up! She had planned on enticing him with a quick blow job to get his mind stimulated again before she informed him of her latest plan to eliminate Jessie.

After not hearing from him for days, she had first become concerned, then annoyed. After all, they had never gone more than a day or two without seeing each other, talking to each other or texting each other. She had called and texted yet he hadn't answered.

The text had asked, no, instructed her to meet him at this seedy ass hotel. Now that he had, it irritated her to no end. First, how dare he demand anything of her after having remained uncommunicative for so long? Even though, the text had cautioned that they had to be more careful for he thought Jessie suspected something was going on between the two of them.

Also, why would Lucas ask her to meet him at such a dump on the outskirts of town? The place was little more than a shack. She eyed the tiny room with its threadbare sheets and filthy mattress. There was a far outdated television that only picked up one channel and a dilapidated dresser. Disdain was etched across her face. Glancing at her watch, Olivia reluctantly took a seat on the dusty chair, but not before giving it a thorough wiping with several Kleenex.

After ten minutes passed, she glanced at her watch again her patience had worn out. "Fuck!" She cursed. Gathering her purse, she was about to head out when the knock on the door gave her pause. Without pretense, she rushed over and snatched it open. "Well...It's about time yo' ass got..." Olivia's words died in her throat upon recognizing that it was Jessie and not Lucas standing before her. She took an involuntary step back. "Jessie!" She clutched her fist together at her throat. "Why are you here? What...What do you want?" She moved back further as Jessie entered the room. Panic welled up in her eyes as he wordlessly turned and closed the door. It wasn't until he turned back that she noticed him holding Lucas's phone. Utter terror began to make its presence known to her.

As Jessie stepped closer, Olivia found herself sitting on the bed and briefly wondered how she'd gotten there. Before she could speak, however, Jessie did. "Hello, Olivia. I know you're surprised to see me. Oh, before you cause your stupid little brain to have a meltdown wondering what happened to your little lover, Lucas will no longer be around to enjoy your pleasures. He's been forever indisposed."

Jessie gave a slight chuckle at the shudder that ran through

Olivia's body. "Oh, don't worry." He continued. "I've made sure that he was well-taken care of for his many years of loyal service to you."

The knowledge of Lucas's plight caused Olivia to get over her initial shock. "What the hell are you doing Jessie? Why are you here and what do you want? Who I choose to fuck ain't none of your damn business!"

Jessie had to admire her gall. Even now, knowing that he knew what she was up too, she still managed to find some way to become upset with him, or at least, pretend to be.

"You know Olivia, you are absolutely right. It's none of my business what snake you choose to let crawl between your legs. But, it is my business when the two of you try to kill me."

Before she could utter a response, Jessie backhanded her so hard, she flew across the bed and landed hard on the floor. When she managed to regain her footing, all thoughts of cursing, running, fighting or anything else, disappeared. Jessie was not standing there alone. Lion had entered the room as well. He, however, paid her no attention. Instead, he busied himself with laying out several objects atop the dresser.

Olivia knew that his actions did not bode well for her. She wanted to protest, to scream, fight or do something, but she couldn't. Terror had it's grip wound tightly about her. Her mind was fuzzy but she forced it to focus on Jessie's words.

"You're going to regret the day that you betrayed me, Olivia. I promise you this." He grabbed her by the wrists before she could even think to protest. In fact, she didn't even know that he could move as fast as he did. As if a lamb being led to slaughter, she just as meekly walked with Jessie. She sat in the chair she had recently vacated.

Before Olivia knew it, Lion had bound her hands and legs. It was then that her mind cleared. She started to scream, thinking that someone in this flea infested trap would hear and call the police. Her screams were cut short as Lion shoved a filthy rag that smelled of urine, deep into her mouth and fixed it with several strips of duct tape. Although she shook her head and tried to fight against the binds, it did no good. Both Lion and the ropes that held her ignored her feeble attempts.

"Now see, I have always hated the way you seem to interrupt me when I'm speaking," Jessie said. "You never really knew when to shut the fuck up or leave me alone. But, don't you worry, I'm going to help you out with that. Now don't worry, I'm not going to kill you. No, see, death is way too good for your trifling ass. After all, you are the mother of my kids. Even though, you're not very good at even being that." Seeing the pleading look in her eyes, Jessie laughed. "Oh, don't trip. I'm going to show you the same amount of mercy you showed to me when you tried to have me killed." He reached over and picked up a butane torch and a sharp knife.

Upon giving Lion a nod, he watched Lion rip the gag from Olivia's mouth, then force her head back. Jessie placed the flame of the torch to the knife. Olivia's eyes bulged as she realized exactly what Jessie had in mind. Before she could do more than release a whimper from her throat, Lion forced his hand into her mouth and pulled violently on her tongue. Jessie in one swift motion severed it. Blood gushed forth, and against all the odds, Olivia let out an ear-splitting wail. It was abruptly cut off as the gag was forced back into her mouth. She could feel her blood as it filled her throat.

"Now see, with that being taken care of, I don't have to hear your lying ass mouth again." Jessie tossed the tongue onto the bed and wiped his hands casually on a damp towel. He took a vise grip and attached it to Olivia's left wrist, on the joint that connected her hand to her arm. As he turned the handle, the grip started squeezing the joint and bone. The pain Olivia experienced was beyond her endurance. She blacked out just as she heard the joint pop and her bone being crushed.

When she was awakened by the vicious blow to her jaw, she knew that she would be crippled for life. Both her ankles and her right wrist had been crushed as well. The pain that throbbed throughout her body was immense.

Olivia wanted so badly to beg and plead for Jessie to stop but that ability had been forever taken away from her. As her eyes rolled, she saw that what she had mistaken for a simple crushing of her limbs, had been incorrect. Both her feet and hands had been completely severed from her body. They lay next to her tongue on the bed. The stubs of her arms and legs were crudely wrapped in surgical gauze.

"Finally decided to rejoin us huh?" Jessie mocked, making Olivia's eyes snap to his face. "Good. You're just in time to watch as I give you an opportunity that you didn't give me. I'm going to allow you the chance to actually not have to hear your own screams."

As Olivia wondered about his words, she watched as Lion handed Jessie a metal bowl filled with a hot liquid. Jessie glared down at her with hatred in his eyes. With one hand, he violently snatched her head to the side. The only thing Olivia knew was the intense pain as the hot liquid wax was poured into her ear. Jessie ignored her muffled screams as he shoved her head to the side and filled her other ear. Instantly, all sounds for Olivia, ceased. That startled her even more so than the pain hurt her. All she could do now was watch in fear as Jessie moved about the room.

Surprisingly, both her sense of smell and eyesight sharpened dramatically. That caused her to see with even more clarity, the red hot two-pronged fork Jessie held in his hand. Olivia screamed even though her voice was gone as Jessie shoved the fork slightly into her right eye. The blinding pain caused her brain to shut down, and her heart to stop. That lasted only as long as it took for Jessie to put out her other eye. It was then that she fainted for the second time.

When Olivia woke, the only thing that functioned on her, was her sense of smell. That sense only allowed her pain fried mind, to realize that the strong aroma that nearly choked her was ammonia. She knew that she lay on the mattress in the hotel. The place had been both stripped clean and sanitized like never before. No one would ever have a clue as to who'd left her in such a state.

CHAPTER 31

Shaniqua thought back on the previous year with pleasure. She and Valentino were like Bonnie and Clyde. Without mercy, they smashed every obstacle that had risen up against them. Shaniqua held no loyalties to anything or anyone. Her aim in life was to climb to the absolute top of the power mountain. Of course, that had been her goal from the start and nothing had given her reason to alter her course. If anything, the things she'd gone through had only intensified her desires. One taste of the wealth that Valentino and his family possessed had been like an intoxicant to her. She longed and hungered for more.

Thinking back, her mind briefly touched on her former friends Tanya and Raena. Shaniqua hadn't seen Tanya since Raena's funeral, not that she cared. Tanya was a permanent fixture in her past. Besides, Shaniqua knew that if she had kept hanging around those two, her star would have never risen. And, even if it had, it would have never risen as high as it was.

Shaniqua relished the fact that everyone in the streets knew her, and not only knew her but actually feared her. After all, she was Valentino's girl. And, no one dared try crossing him. If they did, they knew that a slow and painful death awaited them.

Shaniqua smiled to herself knowing that she was the envy of almost every woman around. She sensed it in the hard looks they gave her, or the whispers behind her back that they thought she hadn't heard And, not just jealousy because she was with Valentino. No, it was also because she was strikingly beautiful and possessed a body that had men drooling all over themselves.

Valentino had insisted that she keep herself in perfect shape. That was one thing he didn't have to worry about. Shaniqua loved the attention. Her body drew far too much of it to let herself go to waste.

Shaniqua double checked her flawless make-up once again before stepping from her brand new Cadillac CTS. It was black with a velvet interior. They seventy-five thousand dollar car had been a gift from Valentino just because Shaniqua had successfully handled a multi-million dollar transaction while he had been called back home by his father. Truth be told, not only had she handled that business, but kept his entire empire running smoothly for the duration of his absence. None of their workers dared to get out of line for they feared her just as much as they feared Valentino.

Stepping smartly, she made her way into the large, spacious office that Valentino had in the right wing of their new twenty million dollar home. The moment Valentino had shown her the place, Shaniqua had fallen in love with it. Along with the office, the mansion boasted five bedrooms, all designed like suites from Chicago's Omni hotel, six and a half bathrooms, a large spacious kitchen, dining room, a den that held a rare collection of first edition novels along with over ten thousand titles. A game room with billiards, dart boards, a fully stocked bar, table tennis, and a ninety-six-inch flat screen projection television and game consoles that could, at the push of a button, call up over two thousand game titles and also allow the user to create his or her own games.

There was also a large patio equipped with a sauna, pool, and jacuzzi, a full-court basketball and tennis court along with an outside bar, a barbeque island that would make any grill master green with envy stood out. There was also a six-car garage that was currently filled. The home sat on five acres of lush green property.

Valentino was deep in discussion over his cell when Shaniqua entered. He gave her a quick smile then continued. It was obvious to her from his tone that he was none too pleased with the other individual on the other side of the conversation. Annoyed, Valentino finally snapped, effectively silencing the other person. He issued cryptic orders rapidly, then ended the call.

Turning to Shaniqua, he scowled, yet not because of her or anything she had done. Walking over, Valentino wrapped his arms around her waist and planted a solid kiss on her lips. "I'm growing extremely annoyed with this Jessie Character." He mumbled into her ear. "He acts as if he does not wish to comply with my plans."

Shaniqua had no need for Valentino to clarify his statement. She was all too familiar with Valentino's plans to move weight on both the east and west sides. After all, she had come up with the details herself. This Jessie had opposed their every move and effort to introduce their product to the local junkies and dealers. Even though they were offering it at a lesser price, all attempts had failed.

Only two weeks ago, six of Valentino's dealers had disappeared, along with their stash. They had resurfaced three days later, or at least parts of them had. Headless torsos, an arm or leg and one, the leader's head was minus the tongue and eyes. There was no mistaking the clear cut message. If Valentino continued to press his luck, just like the street punks, he too would find himself one day, without a head.

Valentino had been so livid, he'd ordered all of Jessie's known spots raided. He'd sent over fifty guys armed to the teeth, with one order; rain down totals destruction.

The city's streets had run red with so much blood. Both the police and the mayor's office had called the bloodbath the most despicable thing that they had ever witnessed. They cautioned the residents to remain vigilant and to report any information they had to the authorities. Since the day of the hit, the two sides had been going back and forth piling bodies with no end in sight.

"Salano is becoming more and more useless each day." Valentino snapped. "Perhaps I should just get rid of his ass now and save myself the trouble of even having to hear his excuses." Valentino didn't see Shaniqua's concerned look; however, he was too intent on his plans to break Jessie.

Although Valentino's father hadn't approved of the way he was handling things, he had reluctantly agreed, after much pleading on Valentino's part, to allow him to do as he pleased. "So long as you get the right results." His father had admonished him. That was exactly what Valentino intended to get.

To cover her sudden lapse at the mention of Salano's name,

Shaniqua turned to the full bar and poured two drinks. She sipped one while handing Valentino the gin and tonic. She had to convince Salano to come up with what Valentino wanted. Shaniqua didn't want to lose her side piece. She and Salano had been regular sex partners since the first day the two of them had met. She knew that Salano was sprung on her, but she held no illusions that if he felt that his life was about to be snuffed out, he wouldn't hesitate to expose their tryst. After all, loyalty to the pussy only went so far and didn't include giving your life up for it.

Turning her mind back to Valentino, Shaniqua moved quickly into his arms. Before he had time to register what she was doing, Shaniqua had his zipper open and was massaging his penis to erection. All thoughts were temporarily extinguished from his mind as she wrapped her lips around the head of his dick, teasing it with her tongue. As she pleased Valentino, Shaniqua's mind was formulating a plan to deal with Salano. She proceeded to give Valentino the best head job he'd ever had.

CHAPTER 32

For Tanya, the past year rushed by in a flash. She sat in her office looking around in quiet disbelief. It was still hard to fathom Raena's death and Tanya knew that she had never gotten over the Loss of Cory. Even as she thought of him, the familiar pain made its presence known in her heart. She both knew and had no desire for that hole to ever be filled.

Picking his photo off her desk, Tanya Looked at it for the thousandth time and thought back on the times they'd shared. She relieved the dream that was his love. They had made so many wonderful memories and Tanya cherished inch and everyone.

After a few moments, she returned the photo to its spot on the desk and tried to force her mind back to the shop's inventory list that was displayed on her computer's screen. It did no good. She had no desire to do any work. Shutting down the computer, she resigned herself to finish it later. After all, the shelves were stocked and business had never been better.

She had to admit, it was actually doing better than she had ever anticipated.

The success of the shop was not the only thing Tanya was proud of. She was also extremely pleased with the way her sexual reassignment surgery had gone. She had taken a month off and flown to Trinidad, Colorado to have it done. Although the recovery had been a painful one, Tanya had welcomed it as if it were an old, long lost friend.

She was more than pleased with the final results. "I got all this pussy and no man to break it in." She said softly to herself. She hadn't even attempted to date anyone since Cory's death. Just the thought of doing so had been like a slap in the face. She felt as if she even tried, it would be a betrayal of his memory.

"Cory wouldn't want me like this." She whispered to herself. She knew her words were true. Cory would want her to be happy; to have a life and to live it to the fullest. He had always said as much to her. He would definitely not want her to mope around alone, lonely and miserable.

Standing suddenly, Tanya left the office and headed to the front of the shop. The place was empty of customers because the shop had closed an hour earlier for the day. Spotting her assistant, Kendra Armstrong, Tanya handed her the day's receipts and a green bank bag with the cash. "I'm going to leave early. Lock up and drop this off at the bank's deposit box. I'll talk to you in the morning." Before Kendra could inquire, Tanya moved through the doors.

Glancing at her watch, Tanya saw that it was a little after 9:00 P.M. She quickly made her way home. Once there, she took a long hot and soothing bath and after feeling the stress and depression of the past year washing off of her, wrapped a towel around herself. She took her time dressing.

Tanya had on impulse, decided to go out on the town. She dressed in a shimmering green silk spaghetti strap dress that clung to her womanly curves and showcased her slender shoulders. A matching pair of heels by Jimmy Choo and a clutch handbag of Ivory hue complemented her dark skin. She wore her hair in loose curls that flowed down her back. A single diamond necklace, matching earrings and bracelet also complimented her look. Tanya touched her throat, bosom and her wrists with her favorite scent and smiled in the mirror at the results.

When she stepped from her Porsche and handed the valet her keys, she smiled at the appraising glance he gave her. After debating on what to do, she had decided to visit the jazz club on the third floor of Gyrations again. She had a moment of reflection as she stepped inside. She recalled when she, Raena and Shaniqua had all come for the first time. Tanya smiled to herself at the brief memory, then pushed it to the back of her mind.

Making her way to the bar, Tanya ordered a caramel apple martini once she'd gotten the bartender's attention. When the drink arrived, she sipped it at one of the bars stools and delightedly relished the taste. Scanning the crowd, she could see that the place was as packed, if not more so than on the night of her first visit. The upbeat sounds of the live band had the dance floor packed. Tanya nodded and swayed in her seat to the sounds.

She had to admit that there were a lot of fine, good looking men in the place. And, they had obviously dressed to impress, yet she didn't find herself drawn to any of them.

After having been there for an hour, she had turned down more offers than she cared to remember. Although she didn't drink much, she was working on her third martini. She also knew that it was her last. After all, she did have to drive home.

Looking up suddenly, Tanya thought she saw a vaguely familiar figure, but as the man in question turned towards her, she knew that she didn't know him. Just as she started to look away, however, recollection hit her. No, she didn't know him, but she had seen him before. In fact, it had been here at this very club the first time she'd visited.

Tanya had been sitting at the table alone and he had been at the one directly across from her. He had been with a woman yet he and Tanya had made eye contact on several occasions. She wasn't sure, but Tanya thought that he had been feeling her. She had also been feeling him, she admitted.

As if her thoughts were drawing him, the guy looked up and directly at her. Tanya saw his eyes squint then grow large as he too recalled her. He quickly made his way over. Extending his hand, he spoke.

"Hello. I'm Jessie." Tanya took his hand into hers. She was surprised at both the smoothness of it as well as the hidden strength it possessed.

"Hello, Jessie. I'm Tanya." She heard herself reply. She released his hand and before he could respond, she contin- ued. "Would you join me and allow me to buy you a drink?" Jessie chuckled, yet took the seat beside her. "What are you drinking?" She asked.

When he told her, Tanya turned to the bartender, who had a slight smirk on his face, and gave him Jessie's order. Moments later, the bartender sat a glass of Patron in front of Jessie. He gave his boss one more look then moved away.

As Jessie took a sip of his drink, Tanya took that moment to check him out. He was absolutely gorgeous in an extremely masculine way. Yet, Tanya sensed more than his beauty. She detected a strong sense of confidence. The same kind of confidence she had felt in Cory yet with Jessie, it was more refined and mature.

There was also an underlining sense of power to him. Tanya knew that he was a man who meant business by just simply looking at him. The way his eyes seemed to briefly move over the crowd, yet Tanya held no doubt that although they moved quickly, they didn't miss a thing. She had seen Cory doing the exact same thing. "So Jessie, exactly what do you do?" She asked in the way of getting the conversation started.

"Well, for one, this club." Jessie laughed. "That and several other businesses that I own." He smiled at Tanya's expression. Holding up the drink, he said. "Thanks." He took another sip. "What about you? What's your occupation?"

"I own a beauty shop and supply store." She replied. There was no mistaking the pride in her voice as she said it. Jessie found that interesting. He loved a self-confident woman. He could sense that Tanya was exactly that and more. He also admired her beauty. She had such an exotic look to her that he found himself breathless each time he looked at her. "You are awe-strikingly beautiful." He said.

Tanya smiled at the compliment. "How would you like to go somewhere a bit more quiet? I would be honored if you allowed me the opportunity to get to know you better." When Tanya nodded, Jessie took her by the hand and led her from the club.

CHAPTER 33

The office Jessie had at the club was beautifully designed. He offered Tanya a seat on one of the plush sofas then seated himself beside her. They both, now that they were alone, seemed at a loss for words. The sounds of the *jazz* band could faintly be heard, yet neither of them truly noticed.

Clearing his throat, Jessie asked if she wished for another drink. Tanya declined. "So why don't you tell me about yourself." She said.

Jessie paused briefly, then proceeded to do exactly that. "Well, I'm a father of two. I have a son, Jackson, whose eight and a daughter, Aniah, whose seven. I am, as I said, an entrepreneur. I own several businesses including both a meat packing and shipping company, a stockyard, two small ranches that raise cattle and a few other ventures. I was born and raised right here. I have no siblings and I'm a very single man."

Jessie paused. He couldn't understand what had gotten into

him. He was usually more tactful when dealing with women, yet it was something about Tanya that had him being more straightforward than he had ever been. "What about yourself?"

"Well...." Tanya started, then hesitated. She knew that she had to be straight up with him. "I too was born here and spent my days running through the streets." She laughed lightly, then continued. "I was raised by my grandmother. My mother threw me out of her house when I was fourteen." A pained look crossed her face. Jessie noticed and instinctively reached over and took Tanya's hand into his. Tanya took comfort in the gesture and continued. "My mother died before the two of us could reconcile."

Looking at his face, Tanya could see the unasked question there. She trembled slightly knowing that she had to tell him. Fear gripped her, yet Tanya shrugged it off.

"My mother did not agree with my choice in life and it drove us apart. See..." Once again, she stopped. She couldn't do it. She didn't know how Jessie would react. She found that she was truly feeling him and wanted to see where things would go with him.

Still, what if he flipped out on her? What if he reacted like so many men were known to do? Tanya didn't think that she could handle it. But, what if he didn't? What if Jessie was an open-minded man? A man like Cory? One who saw her for who she truly was. One who would be willing to accept her. Could she be that lucky of a girl? One who had found two men, gorgeous men at that, who was so accepting?

Noticing her reluctance, Jessie gave Tanya's hand a reassuring squeeze. "Go ahead. You can tell me. After all, we all have things we've done that we are not proud of. I'm not here to judge you. I'm here to get to know you. I want to know you. Everything about you. So, feel free to speak openly and honestly." Jessie found that he truly meant every word he'd said.

Taking a deep breath, Tanya nodded. "Well...See..-I'm a post-op transgender." She quickly said. "I was born physically male." She felt the shock of her words in him as the hand she held tensed. Tanya found herself frozen with fear, yet knew that it was fear of rejection. She looked into his face and saw him warring with his emotions. Before she could say more, however, he spoke.

"A transgender?" He looked closely at her and found himself unbelieving. She was so delicate, so feminine, so beautiful. How could she be transgender? Jessie looked down at the hand that held his. She was so exquisite that he found himself doing a self-examination.

How could he be attracted to a transgender? He didn't know, neither did he deny the truth of his feelings. Likewise, he found that he wasn't upset with the fact that she was. If anything, he was more curious to hear more about her. Refocusing back on Tanya, he asked. "Tell me." That is exactly what she did.

The two of them spent hours sitting on the sofa. Tanya shared with him everything. She talked about growing up being reviled, abused, cursed, hated and bullied because of who she was, yet she told him that none of those things broke her. In fact, they only fueled her desire to be both beautiful and successful.

She spoke of meeting Cory and how he had taken her and shown her a whole new side of life. She was surprised to learn that Jessie knew Cory as well. When she asked how

Jessie assured her that he would tell her in due time. Tanya took him at his word. When she finished by telling him of Raena's death, and her decision to have her surgery, Jessie was nodding his head in understanding.

He gave Tanya a reassuring smile. "Now that, I must say, is a very impressive story. Thank you for trusting me enough to share it. You're even more beautiful than I first believed. I love a woman with courage, strength, and intelligence. The fact that you're fine as hell makes it all the more pleasurable." He rose from the sofa. "Come with me." Jessie took her hand in his and led her through the now nearly deserted club. "I want to share with you more about myself. But, I don't want to do it here." Tanya nodded and allowed him to lead her where he would.

Once outside Jessie led her to the waiting limo. Tanya paused and inquired about her car. Jessie took the ticket stub, gave it to one of his bodyguards and after telling him exactly what to do, assured her that it would be quite safe and more guarded than any other car in the entire state. Tanya laughed at that yet knew that he was not joking.

They rode in relative silence. Jessie was still digesting the things she had shared with him. Every time he looked at Tanya, he couldn't believe that she had been born male. As he examined his feelings, he questioned briefly if he, himself, was gay. He laughed at the absurdity of it. Hell no! He wasn't gay.

In that instant, he realized, truly realized that she wasn't either. She was an absolute woman. More woman, in fact, than many of the females who had actually been born so. Reaching, Jessie took her hand into his once more and instantly felt a thrilling chill course through him. It was the same feeling he'd gotten on the night he'd first laid eyes on

Tanya. His mind had dwelt on her quite often over the past year. Her beautiful chocolate skin, her aura, and energy, it all had been so captivating.

Jessie still recalled how on that night, he had mentally compared Tanya to his date at the time. A date whose name or face he couldn't even remember. In his mind, there truly hadn't been any comparison. Tanya had outshone her hands down. Jessie had wanted to get up right then and introduce himself. Only the fact that he didn't desire to appear so crass, had stayed him.

When the limo pulled to a stop, Jessie took her arm after they'd stepped out of the car. Looking around, Tanya was at first confused. All she saw were trees in every direction. Without giving an explanation, Jessie led her through the thickets. She briefly worried about falling or getting her dress snagged in the darkness, then realized that although there were trees and shrubs crowding them, they were not actually on the path. Likewise, she saw that not only was the path paved, but slightly lit as well by an underground lighting system.

Before she could inquire, they suddenly emerged from the woods and into a vast clearing. Tanya looked around in wonder. They stood atop a Large rise. The lights of the city spread out far below them. Jessie led her over to a bench near the chained off edge and they sat. He smiled at her awed expression as she continued to stare out at the city.

She could see past the downtown high rises and out into the bay beyond. The lights of the yachts, fishing vessels, cruise ships, and personal scooners blazed brightly against the sky's black canopy. When Tanya looked at Jessie bright-eyed, he laughed again. "You like?" Tanya nodded.

Jessie found himself pleased knowing that she enjoyed the view. He realized that her opinion truly mattered to him. He wanted to please her; to keep her smiling. He could see himself becoming addicted to that smile. "Good." He continued. When Tanya took his hand in hers again, Jessie began to open up.

"Now, how about I give you a full account about myself?" He glanced away briefly. He had never been so revealing about himself to anyone. And, especially not upon just meeting them.

He began by talking about his father and how he had struggled and scraped to build his business. Jessie didn't speak of his mother, but nothing but pride and reverence shone in his voice when speaking of Malcolm. He talked about meeting Olivia, the mother of his two children, and of her deception. Where he spoke with reverence about his father, with Olivia, his voice dripped with disdain. He told Tanya of Olivia's betrayals and how he had learned of her cheating. He mentioned how he'd walked in and caught her having sex with the nanny.

Jessie paused as the painful memories came flooding back upon him. It surprised him how much effort it took for him to force the memories away. Still, the pain lingered on. Continuing, he mentioned the death of his father and the hole that still remained in his heart. Tanya nodded her head in understanding, yet remained silent. She had no desire to interrupt him.

Jessie noticed that the night was growing cool. He removed his jacket and placed it over Tanya's shoulders. Tanya smiled gratefully, the scent of his body enveloped her and she inhaled deeply. Her smile increased. She snuggled more tightly into the jacket.

When Jessie continued to speak, his voice took on a more intense tone. He looked at her cooly. "I'm not just a businessman Tanya. I assume that by your association with Cory, you're familiar with the other side of life. The street side. I'm sure you knew what Cory did for a living right?" Tanya nodded. "I thought so. Well...I'm in the business. I handle mine. The reason I'm telling you this is because I want you to know exactly who I am and what I'm about. After all, if you choose to get involved with me, you should know. And, yes, I most definitely want that involvement."

Tanya allowed the meaning of Jessie's words to wash over her. They sent a warmth through her that caused her heart to glow brightly. "I want that in- involvement also." She replied.

Jessie leaned over and kissed her while drawing her close. The sweet taste of Tanya's lips delighted him. He found himself suddenly consumed with desire. It started as a tiny spark deep down inside of him that quickly fanned its way into a soul-consuming blaze. He felt Tanya surrendering into his arms and he wrapped her tightly. He didn't know how long the kiss lasted, but he was slightly disappointed when it came to an end. "Come on." He said helping her to her feet. He wrapped his arms around her and led her back to the waiting limo.

CHAPTER 34

Tanya was amazed at the way she and Jessie were vibing. She often pinched herself just to reassure her mind that she was not living a dream. They had been so caught up in each other, neither noticed the passage of time. That one night had quickly turned into a week, which in turn, turned into over three months. They spent nearly every day in each other's presence. Tanya had effectively turned over the running of the beauty shop To Kendra Armstrong.

Where Cory had opened her eyes to a whole new world, Jessie had open them to an entire universe. Tanya felt like Princess Jasmine in the cartoon, "Alladin." Especially, one night when she and Jessie were flying high above the city in his personal helicopter. When she, at one point, had grown frightened, Jessie leaned over and whispered in her ear. "Don't you dare close your eyes," As he wrapped his arms protectively around her. From that point on, Tanya never did.

They spent the entire month in Sidney Australia, on a sheep farm that was owned by one of Jessie's contacts. Tanya enjoyed the outback and longed to return when it was time for them to leave. Jessie assured her that they would. They flew from New York to Seoul, South Korea and spent two weeks there. They made love the entire time and only ventured out to sightsee when their sexual appetites were sated.

Tanya sat back on the plush sofa and watched as Jessie, Jackson, and Aniah for the children were living with him permanently, ran through the house laughing and playing. Olivia, Jessie told Tanya, had just up and abandoned them one day. He said that she had shown up at his office with them in tow, demanded that he take on more responsibilities and turned and left them without further comment. Tanya couldn't believe the callousness of some people. She knew that were she able to have children, she would cherish them to no end.

Tanya looked up as Jessie entered the room minus the children. She was in his arms before she knew it. That was another thing Tanya loved about Jessie. He was the most affectionate man she'd ever known. He explained to her that it was due to the fact that he never truly believed in love until she'd come into his life. Tanya felt his body reacting to her nearness.

Jessie had a burning passion in his eyes. Leading her by the hand, they quickly made their way to the master bedroom on the second floor. Once there, they wasted no time. Jessie undressed Tanya, admiring her beautiful body as he always did while doing so. Once he had stripped, he lay her down on the bed and took his time savoring her with his tongue. When he tasted her womanhood, she was hot and wet. Her cleft pussy lips throbbed with the sensation his tongue was giving her. Tanya was calling his name and begging for him to take her. Jessie rapidly replied.

Upon entering her tightness, Jessie shuddered with pleasure. Never had he had pussy so exquisite. Tanya remained hot, tight and wet for him the entire time. He was in no rush with his strokes. Time seemed to stand still as they joined themselves to each other.

Their movements quickly became in synch. The first time they had made love, it was both hot and frantic. After all, the two of them had gone without sex for quite some time. Jessie had been elated to be the one who broke her in and in effect, had taken her virginity. He had told her so afterward. Tanya admitted that she was just as thrilled that he was the one who'd done so.

Jessie felt her body begin to quiver and knew the Tanya was on the verge of a climax. He increased his speed, bringing pleasure to both of them. Tanya cried out with the force of her release. Moments later, Jessie joined.

They lay entwined together enjoying the warm sensation of each other's bodies. Jessie smiled and Laughed lightly. When Tanya inquired why he simply smiled again. "I was thinking that maybe Santa Clause and the tooth fairy are real." Tanya had no idea what he was talking about but she knew that in his own way, he had just told her that he'd fallen deeper in love.

CHAPTER 35

Jessie sat in silence watching as his man looked around nervously. He was taking his time digesting the things he'd just heard. Tanya stood near one of the large windows yet she wasn't taking in the view. No, she was staring hard at the man trying to force her mind to recall where she had seen him before. Tanya knew that if she kept at it, it would eventually come to her.

Jessie suddenly looked up. "So this shit is supposed to go down?" He eyed the guy Jessie knew that Spinner was like a double-edged sword. Jessie knew that he worked for Valentino. He had no doubt about it, even though he hadn't confirmed it yet. But, with his suspicions, he made sure that the things Spinner knew or told anyone, was never what was actually in the works.

When Spinner nodded, Jessie rose and took a small stack of bills from the desk and handed it to Spinner. There was ten thousand dollars in the stack. Spinner quickly pocketed the money and when Jessie nodded, he made his way out.

Turning back to Tanya, he raised a questioning eyebrow. Jessie had grown to know her body language and he was sure that she was deep in thought. "What is it, babe?" He asked.

Tanya looked at him and smiled. He never ceased to amaze her. She walked over and stood next to him. Jessie wanted to but resisted the urge to take her in his arms. "I'm trying to figure out where I know that guy from. I know I've seen him before but I...Oh well, it will come to me ." She moved closer to Jessie and he didn't resist.

Tanya melted into his arms. Her mind seemed to always daze over in his presence. Suddenly, she stepped back. "That's it, baby. I know where I've seen him. He was with my friend Shaniqua. They were going out together for a while. I think that was before she started going out with Valentino however."

Jessie nodded. If he needed any more proof that Spinner was being a double informant, Tanya's revelation clarified it. With that in mind, Jessie reexamined Spinner's words. He had told Jessie that Valentino and his men were planning a raid on his meat packing plant. They had obviously found out the true reason Jessie was using the place.

Spinner claimed that the hit was to take place in a week. Something told Jessie that the hit would be taking place sooner. He made a few mental notes and would be sure that he was waiting no matter when the hit went down.

Part of him wanted to just go and confront Valentino straight out. Jessie knew that he held more firepower and men than Valentino, yet he resisted the urge. No, he knew that patience and the element of surprise would work best.

"I'm going to put an end to this shit once and for all baby. I've played around with this fool long enough. He's finally gotten beside himself. Nobody is going to think that they can just walk up and take my shit."

Tanya was nodding her head at Jessie's words. Jessie noticed and pulled her closer once again. "So what do you think baby?" He asked. Tanya remained quiet for some time. She wasn't sure, but something inside was telling her that Shaniqua was involved in some way. Tanya didn't know how, but she knew that it was true.

"I was just thinking about Shaniqua. She's one scandalous ass bitch! You have to really watch her. I know that she's got her hands in this somehow. I can feel it." Tanya said. "Look, daddy, do something for me." When Jessie nodded, she continued. "Have everything moved right now. Shut down the whole thing. That way, when they do try something, won't be nothing there for them to find."

Jessie laughed while nodding. He liked the way Tanya's mind worked. He had already considered doing just that. "Alright baby. I'll shut it down. But, when they do come, I'm going to make sure something is waiting for them." Jessie laughed again.

CHAPTER 36

Shaniqua was more amped about this job than any of the previous ones she'd accompanied Valentino and his men on. She was excited because she knew that with the success of the job, she and Valentino would sail to newer heights. Nothing and no one in the streets would be able to stand in their way. They would have absolute power. Valentino would be the undisputed king of the streets and she, without a doubt, would be the queen.

There was no doubt about the success of the job. She had convinced Valentino to use Spinner as a decoy and to feed Jessie false information. Unbeknown to her, Valentino had known for quite some time that Spinner was working as an informant for Jessie.

Once Spinner had returned, Valentino had killed him right on the spot. Shaniqua had felt a moment of regret, but it soon passed. After all, she would find another replacement for him with no problem. Plus, she still had Salano. Besides, no dick was worth getting in the way of getting her money.

Still, learning of Spinner's double dealings had been a small blow to her sense of pride. Shaniqua got over it immediately, however. She now took satisfaction in knowing that his deception would only aid Valentino in taking down Jessie. As far as he went, although she had never see Jessie, Shaniqua knew that it was far past time for him to be eliminated. She had major plans and Jessie was definitely in the way.

She looked around as Valentino and his men took up their positions around the large meat plant. She was in the background where Valentino insisted she remain. Shaniqua wasn't too fond of that, yet she didn't argue with him. She clutched the gun she held at her side, tightly. She was anxious to get the party started. She knew that Jessie ran a full-scale operation out of the place. The way he was shipping weight all over the country was more than a little impressive.

Shaniqua caught the sudden movement from the corner of her eye. Valentino had given his men the signal to go forward. Within a matter of seconds, about twenty darkly clad figures converged on the building. A sudden, blast rang out loudly as the doors and windows were blown away by the carefully placed explosives. "This is too damn easy. Like taking candy from a baby." Shaniqua whispered to herself.

The moment she'd been hoping for came. Shaniqua rushed into the building only to halt a step behind Valentino. She had expected to find a large scale operation in full swing. What she saw, however, was an empty building. No workers were cooking up product. There were no bricks of cocaine piled high or trucks loaded down with powder. From the looks of things, obviously, Spinner's information had been wrong.

Valentino's men were scattered about looking around in confusion. They waved their weapons about at nothing.

"Shit!" Valentino exclaimed. Before he could give the order to retreat, the fireworks started.

From out of nowhere, bullets began to ring out. His men began dropping to the floor while others scrambled around taking shelter behind whatever offered any form of protection. Valentino snatched Shaniqua down beside him. They lay low behind a large metal freezer. Bullets ricocheted all around them.

The sounds of men screaming in death filled the air along with the smell of burning gun powder. "Stay here," Valentino instructed Shaniqua. He had expected to see fear or panic in her eyes, yet there was none of that. If anything, she seemed to be becoming more excited. Shaniqua nodded and he smiled.

Before she could speak, however, Valentino rushed from behind the freezer's cover guns blazing, and joined his men who were now firing back. Jessie's men had come out into the open. The scene looked like the filming of a movie or something, only the bullets tearing into flesh dispelled the illusion.

Soon, all sense of time was lost. The dying men moaned. Shaniqua couldn't stand not knowing what was going on. When a lull in the gunfire came, she raised her head. The scene stole her breath away. The entire floor of the place was covered in blood and bodies. Fearing the worst, Shaniqua looked around frantically searching for Valentino. Her eyes caught sight of him. He was holding his right arm and pointing his gun at a man standing about ten feet away. From the redness that covered Valentino's fingers, Shaniqua knew he'd been shot. Panic finally hit her.

Without a moment's hesitation, Shaniqua raced from the safety of the locker. Just as she neared the two men, she saw the other man's face. She froze. He was the man she'd seen at the restaurant when she was with Ervin and had seen at the club as well when she was with Tanya and Raena. Even now, he was breathtakingly beautiful.

Was he Jessie? The question popped up unbidden into her mind. Before she came up with the answer, both Valentino and the man spotted her. "Shaniqua get back!" Valentino shouted. Shaniqua didn't respond. Nor, did she run.

The man had her totally captivated. "Shaniqua!" Valentino shouted a second time. His voice finally broke her trance. Just as she started to move, however, Jessie spoke.

"Don't move bitch! I'll blow your fucking head off." Jessie knew exactly who Shaniqua was. Tanya had told him every-thing about her former friend. He knew that she was a snake in the grass. Tanya had spoken of the deception Shaniqua had perpetrated on her friend Raena. To play with someone's life like that was unbelievable.

Shaniqua looked hard at Jessie but ignored his words. Instead, she moved to stand beside Valentino. Both men gave her a sharp look. "Drop the fucking gun." Jessie snapped. When Shaniqua didn't, he pointed his gun at her. Valentino moved over protectively to shield her.

"No. You drop your weapon. In case you can't count, it's two of us against you. Your men are dead fool and you're alone." Valentino said laughing when Jessie looked around the room. No smile crossed his face, however. His eyes blazed with heated anger. Valentino clutched the handle of his gun tightly. "I won't ask you again." Reluctantly, Jessie complied.

"Now that's more like it," Valentino said confidently. A grimace crossed his face as pain shot through his arm.

Shaniqua noticed and would have moved to assist him, but Valentino shook his head no. "It's nothing." He told her.

Shaniqua wanted nothing more than to put a bullet in Jessie right then and there for shooting her man. Only Valentino's voice as he continued to speak to Jessie stayed her hand. "You've caused me quite a lot of problems, but now that's going to come to an end."

Just as he prepared to shoot Jessie, an ear splitting sound filled the room. "Noooooooooo!" All three of them whirled around as Tanya came running up to stand next to Jessie. Shaniqua was so shocked, she nearly dropped the gun in her hand. "No. Don't shoot him." Tanya said. She stared hard at Valentino. She didn't spare Shaniqua a glance. It wasn't until Shaniqua spoke that she did.

"Tanya? What the fuck are you doing here?" She snapped her eyes back and forth between her former friend and Jessie. Suddenly, it hit her like a punch. "What? Are you serious? Don't tell me that the two of y'all are together!" Shaniqua laughed hard then continued. "This shit can't be true." She laughed again. The men didn't speak even though Valentino recognized Tanya as well. He hadn't seen her since the death of Cory.

"Shaniqua. What the fuck are you doing?" Tanya asked. She looked at Valentino. "Why are y'all doing this?" Valentino remained silent, yet Shaniqua couldn't contain her laughter.

"Nigga for real? Are you serious? Why the fuck you think we doing it? For fun? Don't be a dumb motherfucka! We doing it for all of this." She waved her arms around but everyone knew she wasn't referring to the empty meat plant. "We doing it for the power. For money. For all that shit! This nigga here," She pointed at Jessie. "He's in the fucking way and refusing to move. So, we're going to move his bitch ass. It's a damn shame too. I know this shit sucks huh? We done had to off one of yo' niggas already. Now we gone smoke another one. It must really suck to be you."

Everyone knew that Shaniqua was referring to Cory. Her taunts were hate laced. She had never truly gotten over or forgave Tanya or Raena for the way they'd jumped her that night at the club. She decided once she'd offed Jessie, she would knock Tanya's noodles too.

"What! You bitch!" Tanya snapped. "You fucking slutty ass bitch!" She clenched her teeth and would have attacked Shaniqua, gun and all, except Jessie held a restraining arm around her waist. In doing so, he felt the hard steel of the .357 she had tucked behind her back. Jessie kept her in his arms.

"Bitch! You faggot ass nigga! I'm gone bust a cap in yo' ass." Shaniqua raised her gun.

Before she could fire, however, Jessie shoved Tanya to the floor while drawing the gun from her waist. Both Tanya and Shaniqua screamed. Tanya as she hit the floor and Shaniqua in frustration. Jessie dove to the side and fired twice in rapid succession, while at the same time, Shaniqua unloaded as well.

Jessie's first round slammed hard into Valentino's chest sending him flying backward in a spray of blood. The second one caught him just below his hip. When Valentino hit the floor, he lay unmoving.

Both Shaniqua 's and Valentino's bullets struck Jessie hard. One went through his right shoulder just below the collar bone and the other struck him in the lower part of his right side a few inches from his navel. Jessie, like Valentino, lay unmoving in a puddle of blood.

For the moment, both women forgot about each other as they rushed to their men. Shaniqua knelt beside Valentino, yet she could see that he was dead. His eyes stared out at nothing. She screamed her anguish and threw herself across Valentino's body. All rational thoughts fled her mind in the presence of her overwhelming grief.

Tanya was on her knees crying frantically while at the same time, trying to tend to Jessie's wounds. He looked at her with love and tried to speak. No words came forth. Tanya was nearly hysterical, yet something urged her to keep her mind together. Otherwise, she knew that Jessie would die.

"It's going to be okay baby. Just hold on." Tanya pleaded with him. "I'm going to get you out of here. I'm going to get you to the hospital." She looked around and on impulse, grabbed the gun that lay at her feet. She quickly moved behind Jessie and although she didn't wish to move him, pushed him up by the shoulders into a sitting position. Jessie moaned in pain.

"I'm sorry babe but I got to get you up. Can you help me?" Jessie gave a slight grunt and nodded. Tanya placed his left arm around her neck, helping her get him to his feet. She whispered words of encouragement the entire time. All thoughts of Shaniqua and Valentino left her mind. Yet just as soon as she turned Jessie to leave, Tanya froze. Shaniqua was standing over Valentino's body with blood covering her from her neck to her waist. It also dripped from her hands that held a 9mm Glock.

There was no mistaking the wild look in Shaniqua's eyes. Tanya instantly knew that Valentino was dead. She found that she didn't care. Before she could speak, Shaniqua did.

"You bitch! You filthy ass motherfucker! You killed my man." Tanya didn't know if she was speaking to Jessie or her. Shaniqua's eyes were glazed over. "Do you think I'm gone let yo' ass live?" She raised the gun.

"Shaniqua, no!" Tanya heard herself shouting as she raised the gun she held. "Don't do this. Don't make me shoot you. This shit is over. I don't want to have to kill you but..."

"Over!" Shaniqua shouted cutting off Tanya's words. "Bitch it ain't never over! I ain't gone let it be over. Not until you and that nigga you with is dead. Fuck you!"

As Shaniqua aimed once more, Tanya saw with regret that she had no other choice. She raised her own gun. The sudden boom of a round being fired startled her so much, she on instinct, dropped her gun. She expected to feel pain course through her, yet there was none. Tanya hadn't been shot.

Tanya immediately looked at Jessie, yet although he was still bleeding from his previous wounds, didn't seem to have a new one. That's when Tanya looked up and saw Shaniqua crumpled on the floor dead. The back of her head had been blown off. Tanya stared dazed and confused until she heard a voice.

"Well, don't just stand there. We got to get him to the hospital before he bleeds to death." Lion said while shouldering his sniper's rifle. As Lion took Jessie's arm and wrapped it around his shoulder, Jessie let out another low moan.

MPINGO UHURU

Mpingo Uhuru is a transgender author who has written over thirty novels of various genres and numerous short stories.

She is an advocate and activist for transgender rights.

She enjoys nature, reading, playing chess, trivia, sports, and singing.

She is currently hard at work on her next novel.

Mpingo Uhuru